"I've decided not to stand in your way if you want to end things."

Kane almost fell off the fence. "You're not?"

Josie shook her head, albeit sadly. "This was all my fault in the first place—Daddy and the boys forcing you to marry me when you didn't...we didn't...I still haven't..."

Kane tried to relax, but his heart chugged to life. After that, the changes taking place elsewhere in his body made relaxing out of the question.

"I want you to know I'm sorry. I only did it because I wanted you to be my first lover. I still want you to be my first lover, but I'm not going to force anything on you that you don't want."

Kane didn't know how long he'd been staring at Josie's mouth, but as he watched her lips move, he knew she'd never have to force him to do anything. Because he suddenly found himself wanting to kiss her, long and slow and deep, over and over and over.

Dear Reader,

July brings you the fifth title of Silhouette Romance's VIRGIN BRIDES promotion. This series is devoted to the beautiful metaphor of the traditional white wedding and the fairy-tale magic of innocence awakened to passionate love on the wedding night. In perennial favorite Sandra Steffen's offering, *The Bounty Hunter's Bride*, a rugged loner finds himself propositioned by the innocent beauty who'd nursed him to health in a remote mountain cabin. He resists her precious gift...but winds up her shotgun groom when her father and four brothers discover their hideaway!

Diana Whitney returns to the Romance lineup with *One Man's Promise*, a wonderfully warmhearted story about a struggling FABULOUS FATHER and an adventurous single gal who are brought together by their love for his little girl and a shaggy mutt named Rags. And THE BRUBAKER BRIDES are back! In *Cinderella's Secret Baby*, the third book of Carolyn Zane's charming series, tycoon Mac Brubaker tracks down the poor but proud bride who'd left him the day after their whirlwind wedding, only to discover she's about to give birth to the newest Brubaker heir....

Wanted: A Family Forever is confirmed bachelor Zach Robinson's secret wish in this intensely emotional story by Anne Peters. But will marriage-jaded Monica Griffith and her little girl trust him with their hearts? Linda Varner's twentieth book for Silhouette is book two of THREE WEDDINGS AND A FAMILY. When two go-getters learn they must marry to achieve their dreams, a wedding of convenience results in a *Make-Believe Husband*...and many sleepless nights! Finally, a loyal assistant agrees to be her boss's *Nine-to-Five Bride* in Robin Wells's sparkling new story, but of course this wife wants her new husband to be a *permanent* acquisition!

Enjoy each and every Silhouette Romance!

Regards,

Joan Marlow Golan

Joan Marlow Golan
Senior Editor Silhouette Books

Please address questions and book requests to:
Silhouette Reader Service
U.S.: 3010 Walden Ave., P.O. Box 1325, Buffalo, NY 14269
Canadian: P.O. Box 609, Fort Erie, Ont. L2A 5X3

VIRGIN BRIDES

THE BOUNTY HUNTER'S BRIDE

Sandra Steffen

Silhouette
ROMANCE™
Published by Silhouette Books
America's Publisher of Contemporary Romance

For my sister-in-law, Rose, whose name suits her so
perfectly, and who was married to my brother, Ron, for
nineteen years and helped make him a lucky man.

And for their children, Eric, Kurt and Kara, who are all
delightful combinations of their parents.

Because of the four of them, the rest of us are a little
luckier, too.

 SILHOUETTE BOOKS

ISBN 0-373-19306-8

THE BOUNTY HUNTER'S BRIDE

Books by Sandra Steffen

SANDRA STEFFEN

Creating memorable characters is one of Sandra's favorite aspects of writing. She's always been a romantic, and is thrilled to be able to spend her days doing what she loves—bringing her characters to life on her computer screen.

Sandra grew up in Michigan, the fourth of ten children, all of whom have taken the old adage "Go forth and multiply" quite literally. Add to this her husband, who is her real-life hero, their four school-age sons who keep their lives in constant motion, their gigantic cat, Percy, and her wonderful friends, in-laws and neighbors, and what do you get? Chaos, of course, but also a wonderful sense of belonging she wouldn't trade for the world.

Dear Reader,

Ah, life. It's made up of thousands of firsts. First birthdays, first words, first steps, first loves. But I don't think there's a more memorable first for a man or a woman than the first time he or she makes love, for it marks the end of the innocence we call virginity, and the beginning of a person's sexual awakening. Oh, what an ending and beginning it is! Ancient civilizations held ceremonies for such occasions. Modern man's ceremonies might be more private, but in this book Josie McCoy still hears the beat of those ancient drums, still feels the heat of those fires. This feisty, witty young woman plans to make her first time memorable. Now, if she can just get her wounded, bounty-hunter husband to cooperate.

Speaking of cooperating, when my editor called and gave me the opportunity to write a book for Silhouette's VIRGIN BRIDES series, I jumped at the chance to cooperate. *The Bounty Hunter's Bride* is my fifteenth book for Silhouette, and while I've enjoyed writing every one, Josie's story is my favorite. For you see, when those drums started beating for Kane and Josie, I couldn't help but remember…

Here's to happy reading and happy memories!

Always,

Sandra Steffen

Chapter One

There was pain. There was darkness. And there was snow. Kane Slater had lost track of how long his life had consisted of those three stark realities. One hour? Four? Ten? Had there ever been anything else? He knew the sky was up. Therefore, that's where the darkness and the snow had to be coming from. The pain, on the other hand, was coming from all directions: from the sting of the wind on his face, the prickling numbness in his feet and the piercing ache in his shoulder.

He'd tracked men through higher mountains than these, in worse blizzards, but at the time he hadn't been freezing, or bleeding, or lost. Taking as deep a breath as he could without moving his shoulder a fraction more than he had to, he pulled one foot out of the deep snow and took a tortuous step.

There was pain.

He took another step. *There was darkness.*

He drew in another slow, careful breath. *There was snow.*

Pain. Darkness. Snow. Pain. Darkness. Snow. And a flickering yellow light.

A yellow light? He breathed too deeply, clutched his arm and nearly blacked out. Being more careful, he strained to see through the blinding snow. High on the next ridge, a light flickered. Maybe he could make it to that light before he died. Or maybe he was already dead and was having one of those out-of-body experiences and was being drawn up toward that light. Not likely. He had a pretty good idea which direction he was going when he died. And it wasn't up.

He'd never planned to grow old, but by God, he didn't plan to bleed to death on some nondescript little mountain in Tennessee, either. He closed his eyes. Since the light was still there when he opened them again, he concentrated on putting one foot in front of the other.

Blasted blizzard. Blasted weakness. Blasted poor excuse for a mountain.

Josie McCoy stopped humming long enough to open the door on the woodstove and add two more logs to the glowing coals. The fire crackled and popped, the flames curling upward like a living, breathing being that gobbled up wood in exchange for blessed, glowing heat. She closed the door and latched it securely before turning in a circle inside the old hunting cabin high on a narrow bluff in the Blue Ridge Mountains.

The wind whipped snow against the single windowpane. "You know Mother Nature is only doing this out of spite." She spoke out loud and—since there was no one else to talk to—to herself. Her father and the boys were probably having a good belly laugh right about now at her expense. "Go ahead and laugh," she said as if they could hear her halfway down the mountain.

The howling of the wind was her only answer. Peering out the window, Josie smiled, because it was answer enough. J.D., the brother closest to her in age, had claimed she'd never make it two whole weeks with nobody to talk to. Hah! They'd never make it two whole weeks without somebody to cook their meals and wash their clothes and haul their big feet out of the way in order to tidy the place up a little. Her father and brothers might have been mountain men, but thanks to the satellite dish on the shed's roof, the twentieth century had finally made it all the way to Hawk Hollow, Tennessee. Right on its heels had come women's lib. That's what Josie was doing. Liberating herself from those ingrates who were her closest relatives.

"Men!" she sputtered. "With their chew and whiskers and clodhopper boots. Who needs 'em?"

Closing her eyes, she ran her fingers over her face, spreading them wide into her hair, over the collar of her flannel shirt, and—slowly—down to her waist. Surely all men weren't like her father and older brothers. Surely there was one man out there—somewhere—who was tall and debonair and pleasing to the eye. And sexy. She opened only one eye and fixed it on her bed. God, yes, he would have to be sexy.

A log popped, making her jump. Shivering against a sudden draft, she folded her arms, eyed the dwindling stack of logs piled next to the stove and promptly headed for the front stoop where she'd had the good sense to heap enough firewood to make it through the night.

Bracing herself for the shock of the wind, she tugged on the latch. The door swung open with so much force it banged against the wall. A shock went through Josie, but not from the wind. A man stood on her doorstep. A big man. She didn't have time to scream. She barely had time to break the man's fall before he hit the floor, unconscious or dead, she couldn't be sure.

She put all her weight into pushing his legs out of the way so she could close the door. He groaned, and for the first time she saw that his shirt was covered in blood. Gliding down to her knees, she leaned over him and placed a hand on his chest to see if he was breathing. His chest rose slightly beneath her palm. By the time her gaze made it to his face, his eyes were open and he was watching her.

"Who are you?" she whispered.

"Slater. Kane. Slater." His breath caught between each word, and then, before her eyes, he lost consciousness.

"What am I supposed to do with you, Slater Kane Slater?" She lifted the soiled lapel of his sheepskin coat. Swallowing, she closed her eyes for a moment and tried to calm her churning stomach. Growing up with four older brothers, she'd seen her share of blood over the years, but this was the first time in her twenty-three years she'd seen a wound like this all the way through a man's shoulder.

"Lordy, mister," she mumbled after retrieving a threadbare towel from the table and pressing it over both sides of the wound. "I came up here to get away from the men in my life and I sure as shootin' don't need the likes of you bleeding all over my floor."

"Tracks. Snow. Got away."

His voice was harsh and raw and so unexpected that she jumped back in surprise. He let out a long, audible breath and fought against her hand that was pressed over the blood-soaked towel, as if somewhere in his befuddled mind he thought he was still in danger. The next thing she knew he'd rolled to his knees and was staggering to his feet.

Josie rose more slowly. If his eyes hadn't drilled her to the spot, she would have taken a giant step backward. He was tall. Even bleeding he was formidable. He had the face of an outlaw, four or five days' worth of whiskers, skin that looked tough and chapped. His hair was matted to his head. Clean, it would probably be light brown. His eyes were light brown, too. At the moment, they looked kind of crazed.

Gauging the distance between him and the corner where she kept a shotgun handy just in case, she said, "I hope that look in your eyes is from pain and blood loss and not because you're a lunatic. I mean, you're not an escaped prisoner or a murderer or a rapist, are you? Although I doubt that even a crazed lunatic could do much damage in your condition."

The baffled expression that crossed his features came as no surprise to Josie. All men looked at her that way every now and then. "Well?" she demanded. "Are you?"

"Never been to prison. Not a murderer or rapist." He started to sway.

Since he would be a lot easier to maneuver on his feet, she tucked her shoulder underneath his arm to steady him. She staggered beneath his weight. "Whoa, big fella." In an effort to keep him upright, she locked her spine and wrapped one arm around his waist. His arm slid limply down the front of her, the back of his hand brushing her breast.

"Don't have much in the curve department, do ya?"

This time her huff was mostly affronted pride. Slowly, jerkily, she started toward the bed on the far wall. With two more steps to go to make it to the bed, she gritted her teeth and ground out, "A gentleman would never say such a thing."

He fell onto the lumpy mattress, the sudden jar eliciting a raw-sounding oath from his dry lips. Their gazes met, held, his throat convulsing on a swallow she assumed was from the need to cry out in pain. Instead, in a voice that was deep and shaky, he murmured, "It would be a mistake to think of me as a gentleman."

Eyes closed, he sank into unconsciousness once again.

For what might have been the first time in her life, Josie was struck speechless. Staring at the grim line of his lips and the gray pallor of his skin, she finally said, "Just my luck. I finally have an interesting man in my bed and he's half-dead and God only knows what side of the law he's on."

Wondering what on earth he'd been doing out on a night like this, she tried to decide what to do. The fresh blood soaking into his shirt propelled her into action. No matter what he'd been doing, it looked as if it was up to her to save him.

She started with his shoulder. After applying another clean towel over the entry and exit wounds of what could only be the result of a bullet, she reached for a scissors. When he groaned in his sleep, she said, "I know, I know. Bear with me for a few more minutes until I get you out of these soggy clothes."

With shaking hands, she cut his coat and shirt away from his wounded shoulder, painstakingly sliding the wet garments from his body. The sight of a man's bare chest was nothing new to her. Her brothers traipsed around the house without their shirts most of the summer. The McCoy boys were thin and wiry, their chests as hairy as apes. Kane Slater's chest was broad and far from hairy, his stomach muscles forming interesting ridges that disappeared beneath the waistband of faded jeans.

"You're a strong one, aren't you? Well, mister, it's a good thing because I don't think a weaker man would have made it this far. I don't know if it was good luck or the good Lord, but either way it looks as if it's up to me to take it from here."

She doubted he could hear her, but talking calmed her nerves. "Yes, indeedy, you're gonna feel a whole lot better when we get you out of these wet clothes."

It took her five minutes and a considerable amount of huffing and puffing to remove his soggy cowboy boots, and five more to get him out of his jeans. She hesitated a moment after that, uncertain how to go about removing his underwear without injuring his pride.

Squeezing her eyes shut, she curled her fingers beneath the elastic waistband and tugged. Other than getting stuck here and there, the garment came off without too much trouble. For some reason, her breath caught in her throat and her mind turned a little fuzzy. Something strange was taking place deep inside her. It felt a little like the flutter of butterfly wings or daisy petals ruffling on a gentle breeze. If the sensation would have settled any higher, she would have blamed it on hunger. If this was hunger, it was a kind she'd never felt before.

The stranger groaned again. Dropping the last garment of clothing to the rough plank floor, she muttered, "You're a wicked, wicked woman, Josie McCoy. This man has lost a lot of blood and is in terrible pain and all you can think about are the changes takin' place in your own belly."

Without another word, she covered him with a quilt she'd warmed by the stove. He sighed, and dang if something else didn't shift inside her.

"There, there," she murmured. "That's it. Let the heat soak into you. See? It's better without the wet clothes, isn't it? I'm afraid I ruined your shirt and coat getting 'em off you, but everything else came off real smooth. And I didn't linger any longer than absolutely necessary." She glanced at the shape of his body covered by the quilt, and then at the clothes heaped on the floor, thinking that as long as she never had to swear to that on a stack of bibles she'd be okay.

She kept up a quiet vigil the next several hours, talking to him in a soft, reassuring voice. At least it reassured her. The bleeding had finally stopped, and although his color wasn't very good, his breathing was deep and steady and he seemed to be resting more comfortably. Once every hour, she cradled his head in her arm and held a cup of cool mountain water to his lips. He drank several swallows before falling into a deep sleep once again.

Every now and then he mumbled in his sleep. Most of the time she couldn't understand what he was saying, but she answered him anyway, telling him about people he couldn't possibly know and a life he probably didn't give two hoots about. She didn't mention the butterfly wings that had fluttered deep in her stomach, but she wondered what they meant. Maybe it was excitement, or maybe it was an answer to her prayers.

A long time after midnight, his speech became less slurred and his gibberish began making more sense. Wringing out a washcloth over a pan of water she'd heated on the stove, she sat on the edge of the bed and leaned close to him. Placing one hand beside his pillow for balance, she smoothed the warm cloth over his face with long, gentle strokes.

"Warm breezes," he murmured. "Big skies. It's Montana, Ma. Good to be home."

"Montana," Josie whispered. "Home. Sleep now, Kane. Shh. Sleep."

He pressed his face into her hand, sighing as if her touch was all he needed. Josie swore her heart climbed higher in her chest and slowly turned over.

Dazedly she found her feet. She lifted the cloth away from his cheek but she couldn't seem to pull her gaze away from his face. His eyelashes were long—men had all the luck—his eyebrows were thick and straight and sandy brown in color. His nose was straight and broad, like the rest of his features. Sleeping, he looked less formidable, but not less complex. She tried to blame the changing rhythm of her beating heart on the wistfulness she'd heard in his voice. It might have worked if those butterfly wings hadn't started fluttering stronger than ever.

She took one step away from the bed and then another. Still, she didn't take her eyes off him. Placing one hand over her heart and the other low on her stomach, understanding dawned.

"So this is how it feels to be falling in love."

Funny, she'd given up on the whole prospect of love, telling herself she would settle for honest to goodness attraction. She'd had no idea the two sensations were so closely related.

"Mister," she said. "I mean, Kane, honey, it looks like this is our destiny. You're probably gonna want to repay me for saving your life. It turns out this is your lucky day, because I know exactly what you can do to make us even."

Catching sight of her grin in her reflection in the dark window, she set about getting ready for bed. She heated more water, donned a warm nightgown and thick wool socks. Finally, after tending the fire and checking on Kane one last time, she curled up on a wooden bench she'd padded with layers of blankets, and closed her eyes.

The wind was still blowing, but it had lost its roar. She could hear the crackle of the fire and the steady sound of Kane Slater's breathing. *Kane Slater.* She liked the way his name curled through her mind, but she wondered what kind of a man she'd fallen in love with. After all, most men didn't traipse through a blizzard with a hole in one shoulder. Kane had said he was no gentleman. What did that make him?

She pursed her lips, remembering how wistful his voice had sounded when he'd mentioned Montana and warm breezes and his mama. Surely a man who loved big sky country and his mother couldn't be all bad, although she'd read somewhere that even men on death row had a soft spot in their hearts for their mothers. Her instincts told her she would never fall in love with someone who was evil. Those instincts had always been trustworthy before. But she just didn't know. How could she? She'd never been in love before.

As far as she knew, he didn't realize he was here. It was highly likely that he didn't even know where *here* was. They hadn't exactly met under normal circumstances. What did she really know of him? He'd staggered into the cabin, hurt and bleeding, only to fight against the very hands that were helping him. He'd insulted her lack of curves and admitted that he was no gentleman.

Okay, she knew he was strong and gruff and wounded. Pulling the scratchy blanket up around her neck, she sighed. Closing her eyes, she hoped Kane Slater had a gentle side.

"Where in the hell are my clothes?"

Kane's bellow brought Josie awake so quickly her vision blurred. Groggy, she sat up and glanced out the window. No wonder she was a little addle minded. The sky was just beginning to turn gray, which meant she'd been sleeping on the hard bench for less than three hours.

"I asked you a question, dammit."

The room was chilly in the dawn's early light, the fire awfully low. A firm believer in first things first, she swung her feet onto the cold floor and saw to the fire, thinking that Kane Slater's gentle side—if he had one—was going to need a little work.

His rough side, on the other hand, was blatantly apparent. He was sitting up in bed, glaring at her, fresh blood soaking the bandage she'd changed hours earlier. Wrapping a woolen blanket around her shoulders like a shawl, she planted her hands on her hips and glared back. "The clothes I could salvage are over there soaking in a bucket of water. If you hold still, we might be able to get that bleeding stopped again. Or you can sit there and holler and move around until you pass out again. It's up to you."

Kane cradled his right arm and held very still. It took a lot to make him bite back a scathing retort. The little scrap of a woman studying her thumbnail a few feet away had done it without batting an eye. Keeping her in his line of vision, he sank into the pillows at his back and gritted his teeth against the pain shooting through him.

Doing everything in his power to focus on something other than the pain, he studied the woman. Or was she still a girl? A woman, he decided, although it was hard to tell with that blanket wrapped around her. She had straggly blond hair and plain gray eyes that were too big for her narrow face. He wondered what she would look like dressed. While he was at it, he wondered what she would look like undressed. A vague memory hovered at the edge of his mind. He glanced at the back of his hand, and then at the slight slope of her breast. The skin on his hand prickled with a message that short-circuited before it reached his brain.

"You live up here?" he asked.

With a shake of her head that sent her hair tumbling into her eyes, she said, "I live halfway down the mountain in a little town called Hawk Hollow. I came up here to be by myself. It's lucky for you my father and brothers are such narrow-minded fools.''

Kane didn't come close to following her logic. He didn't see what her father and brothers had to do with him, but he supposed she was right about one thing: He *was* lucky he'd stumbled upon this cabin when he did. He was lucky the place had been warm, and he was lucky somebody had been here to get him into bed and make him as comfortable as possible. Although he hated to admit it, he supposed he had to admit that he was lucky to be alive.

Studying the narrowness of her shoulders and the thin body underneath the blanket and thick flannel gown, he said, "You must be stronger than you look if you managed to strip a man my size."

"You are a big one, Kane, that's for sure. And you're right. I'm stronger than I look."

Her smile hit him right between the eyes. He hadn't realized he'd closed them until he tried to wrestle them open again.

"It's okay, Kane," she whispered, placing a hand on his good shoulder. "Relax. That's it. Just rest and think about the things you like."

Her hand was warm and narrow and surprisingly soft where it rested on his bare skin. He liked the touch of her hand, and the sound of her voice, and the way she said his name. "I'm afraid I'm at a disadvantage," he murmured through the darkness swirling toward him from every direction.

"What disadvantage is that?" she whispered.

"You've seen me naked and I don't even know your name."

"I guess we're just going to have to even things up a little now, aren't we?"

His eyes popped open all by themselves. Something that

had no business stirring in a dying man stirred low in Kane's body. His eyes delved hers as she tucked the quilt under his chin.

Holding his gaze, she said, "My name's Josie McCoy. You didn't really think I'd strip down right here and now, did you?"

Kane closed his eyes, wondering when his thoughts had become so transparent. "Can't blame a man for being disappointed."

"Mister. I mean Kane, I'd be disappointed if you weren't disappointed."

His mind was fogging up, making it difficult to concentrate. Just in case he didn't wake up again, he said, "I don't know if you saved my life or made dying easier. I owe you either way."

Moments before the darkness claimed him, her voice came one more time, far, far away. "I'm not going to let you die, Kane, and don't worry. I have every intention of allowing you to repay me. We might have to do a little bartering. We'll talk more when you're stronger."

Bartering? he thought, slipping into that warm, dark place where there was no pain. Images, erotic, hazy and fanciful, shimmered through his mind. Maybe he was dreaming. No, Kane Slater never dreamed.

Something told him he wasn't dying, either. And he had Josie McCoy to thank for it. There was obviously more to her than met the eye.

"You're really a modern-day bounty hunter?"

Kane did his best to keep the growl deep in his throat from escaping. He didn't nod his head for fear that the razor in Josie's hands would do serious damage to his face. Not that he would have minded a scar. It was more pain he was trying to avoid.

"Yes," he grumbled when she lifted the razor from his flesh. "That's what I said."

"Why?"

"What do you mean why?" Teeth clenched, he held perfectly still as the razor made a clean pass along the edge of his jaw.

Swishing the razor in a pan of warm water, Josie said, "Why would a man who claims to have an undying devotion to the great plains and majestic mountains of Montana traipse off in the middle of the night to places unknown? Pistol drawn, you kick doors down and get lost in mountains you say aren't really mountains during blizzards and God only knows what else. My daddy always says everybody's got a reason for doing what they do. Believe me, he knows what he's talkin' about. Why?"

The razor had made four more passes down Kane's face before he'd figured out what her "why?" pertained to. This time there was no stopping the growl from erupting from his throat.

Two nights ago he'd fleetingly wondered if there might be more to Josie McCoy than met the eye. There was more to her, all right, and every last bit of it was driving him crazy. When she wasn't singing, she was talking, and when she was talking, she was usually asking questions. She asked them while she was putting wood on the fire, while she stirred something in a big pot on the stove, while she fed him warm broth and sweetened tea. Kane hated sweet tea. He hated talking and singing. He hated answering questions most of all.

He knew better than to bite the hand that fed him. His shoulder still hurt like a son of a gun, but the wound was starting to heal. It was too soon to tell if there'd been any nerve damage, but at least the bullet hadn't hit a major artery. Still, he'd lost a lot of blood, and it was going to take a while to regain his strength. God help him, he needed his strength to keep from telling Josie what she could do with her tea and her songs and her never-ending string of questions.

"Do you have people frantic with worry over you?" she asked.

"People?"

"You know. A wife, kids, parents."

The razor landed in the metal pan of water with a loud plop. Leaning back, Kane closed his eyes, listening to the scrape of the pan as she slid it away from her across the wood floor.

"No," he said. "No wife, no kids, no parents. Karl Kennedy, the head of the bail enforcement agency in Butte is probably wondering whether I'm dead or alive, but he's wondered that before and won't get real concerned for another week or two."

"Is he going to be upset that your bail jumper got away?" Josie asked.

"Not half as upset as I am. This guy wasn't just a bail jumper. He tried to kill me. Not that I'd ever be able to prove it."

"Then you didn't actually see him shoot you?"

"I got my first inkling about the same time the bullet was kissing my shoulder goodbye."

"That's not funny," she murmured, closer to his ear than he'd realized. "Here. Put this over your face for a few minutes."

She placed a hot, wet towel in his left hand and slowly lifted it to his face. Moist heat seeped into his skin, his groan turning into a deep, contented moan. "Ah, Josie, if you need something to do when you're a little older, maybe you could bring back the old-fashioned shave."

"What do you mean when I'm a little older? I'm already

a grown woman. Why, back in Hawk Hollow I'm considered an old maid.''

She lifted the towel from his face. He opened his eyes, fighting an uncustomary urge to grin. Josie was leaning over him, her gray eyes flashing, her lips parted in indignation. She had a personality big enough for ten women, but there wasn't much to the rest of her. Her light blond hair was tied back in a lopsided ponytail. Her skin was unlined and smooth. Without a stitch of makeup, she looked about thirteen.

Shaking his head, he said, ''You're not old enough to be an old maid.''

''I'm twenty-three.''

''You are?''

''I look younger, I know. I think it's because I'm on the thin side. Dripping wet I barely weigh a hundred and ten.''

The lift of his eyebrow must have made her feel guilty, because she said, ''Okay, a hundred and five.''

Kane didn't want to think about what she would look like dripping wet. He didn't want to think about the fact that she was older than she looked and therefore of legal age. He didn't want to think about how close she was and how alone they were, and, aw, hell. ''Josie,'' he said, exasperated, ''women lie about weighing too much, not too little.''

''I can lie about anything I want to lie about. But I really am twenty-three. How old are you?''

Questions. Always more questions. ''Thirty-four.'' His answer was thin and hollow and as worn as his patience.

''So, you're a thirty-four-year-old bounty hunter from Montana. No wife. No kids. No parents. Do you have any brothers or sisters?''

Leaning his head back, he closed his eyes. Maybe if he went to sleep she would stop talking.

"Well, do you?"

Then again, maybe she wouldn't. "Two brothers. Trace and Spence."

"Only two? I have four. Billy, James, Roy and J.D. They're the main reasons I came up here. That, and I wanted a little time to myself to think. Do you ever need time to yourself to think, Kane? What am I saying? You must have all kinds of time to think when you're not breaking down doors and collecting bounty money. What else do you like to do? Back in Montana, I mean. Just a minute. I'll be right back."

She bustled away to the stove where a kettle of water was beginning to boil. Kane welcomed the reprieve. All these questions were making him feel naked. Of course, he was naked.

He was a grown man, yet he'd slept like a baby most of the past two days. He hated being helpless and he hated being weak, but until his shoulder healed and he regained the use of his right arm and he was strong enough to make it down the mountain, he was at Josie's mercy. The shave, shampoo and bath had been her idea. He was the first to admit they'd felt good, and the first to admit that he was an ornery cuss most of the time. It was an effective tool in holding people at a distance. Josie didn't seem to mind. Hell, she didn't even seem to notice.

He could tell by the soft thud of her shoes that she was nearing. Turning his head, he watched as she stopped at the edge of the ancient bathtub and promptly added the water she'd heated on the stove. Before he'd gotten in, she'd stirred some sort of healing agent into the water, making it milky white and impossible to see through. Breathing in the steam rising from the surface of the water, Kane felt himself relaxing. "Okay, Josie," he said, drowsy from the blessedly warm water. "I can take it from here."

The sound of her hand gliding through the water brought him instantly wide-awake. "What the hell do you think you're doing?" Forgetting his injury, he reached blindly for her hand, only to wince in pain.

"There. See what happens when you try to do things yourself? And I'd appreciate it if you wouldn't swear. It's not as if you have anything I haven't seen before. I'm the one who got you out of your clothes the first night you were here, remember? Besides, you're not the only male I've ever seen naked. Billy's two-year-old runs around with nothing on half the time. Daddy's always yellin' for somebody to put some pants on that boy. You're gonna like my daddy. Just you wait. His name's Saxon. I swear to God I'm not making that up. Shoot. I just lost the soap. Hold on, I'll find it."

Kane was all set to tell her that in case she hadn't noticed there were a few differences between him and her two-year-old nephew, but her fingers skimmed something that most definitely was not the soap, and he forgot what he was going to say. Josie, on the other hand, didn't even miss a beat in her story.

"I have to say I don't think much of their taste in men. Why, my father and brothers want me to marry Obadiah Olson."

Deciding that for once it might be best to keep her talking until he could get things under control, he said, "Obadiah?"

"Obie for short."

"And you don't want to marry Obie?" Kane asked.

"Heavens, no."

"Do you have a reason?"

"He lies through his tooth."

Kane surprised himself by laughing. "Then what do you want? If it isn't to marry Obie and his tooth?"

She brought her hand out of the water, her thumb moving over the soap in a most tantalizing way, wiping out every last bit of progress he'd made below the water's surface. Her face was close to his, moisture clinging to her cheeks. She was on her knees, her elbows resting on the edge of the bathtub. The top two buttons of her shirt were open, awarding him a clear view of her throat and the delicate ridge of her collarbone. Lower, he could make out the outline of one perfectly shaped breast.

Without conscious thought, he lifted his left hand out of the water and slowly raised it. Her face was so close to his he could hear the sound of her breath catching in her throat. Her eyes were the color of dawn. Her lips were full and moist and unmoving.

Will wonders never cease.

He almost commented on her silence, but his hand came into contact with the soft fabric of her shirt, and he didn't feel much like talking. A heartbeat later he knew he was going to kiss her. And then his mouth was covering hers. Her lips were warm and soft and the tiniest bit trembly. She kissed him back, but tentatively, as if she wasn't sure what to do. Kane couldn't remember the last time he'd kissed a woman who didn't take over, who didn't push for more, who simply seemed to savor what was happening at that very moment.

It was a heady sensation, one that wiped out all but the last shreds of coherent thought. Burying his fingers in the loose fabric at her throat, he finally drew away slightly, ending the kiss.

A man had to be careful what he said at a time like this, because there wasn't a lot of blood left above his shoulders. Breathing deeply, he murmured, "I feel a little sorry for poor Obie."

The air whooshed out of Josie, the area surrounding her

heart turning to mush. She'd been experiencing those butterfly sensations on and off for two days, but she'd been
questioning the possibility that she could *really* have fallen
in love with a man she barely knew. She'd begun to wonder
if she'd imagined her feelings for him. She wasn't imagining them now.

She'd known Kane was looking inside her shirt. If he'd
been any other man, her first instinct would have been to
cover herself. But Kane wasn't any other man, and she'd
held her breath, waiting. When his hand had come out of
the water, those old butterflies had fluttered in anticipation
of his touch. Rather than touching her breast, he'd kissed
her, drawing the lapels of her shirt together at the same
time. He might have claimed he was no gentleman, but she
knew differently. And she knew, without a doubt, that her
love for him was real, which brought her to the brink of
what she wanted to say.

Lathering up the washcloth, she smoothed it over his left
shoulder, slowly moving it across his chest. His muscles
flexed beneath her hand, his voice little more than a husky
rasp as he said, "I'll take it from here, Josie. You've already done more than I'll ever be able to repay."

She relinquished the washcloth to him, saying, "I've
been wanting to talk to you about that, Kane."

His eyes narrowed, his hand stilling. "About what?"

She cleared her throat and swallowed the knot that had
formed around her voice box. "About repaying me."

"You want money?"

She shook her head. "No. But there is something you
can do."

"And what might that be?" His voice had taken on an
ominous ring in the silent room.

She'd been rehearsing this for two and a half days. Suddenly she didn't know how to begin. Calling on the angels

for courage, she looked directly into his eyes and said, "I've been dreaming of getting off this mountain for as long as I can remember. If what you said is true and you want to repay me, I'd like you to take me with you back to Montana. I could do almost anything you asked. I'm a virgin, but I'm a fast learner."

Chapter Two

"You're a what?"

Kane yelled too loud and moved too fast. One hurt his eardrums and the other sent pain shooting through his shoulder. He didn't care. It beat the wounded look crossing Josie's face that very instant.

"I'm a fast learner," she said, lowering her eyes.

That wasn't what he'd asked her to repeat. She'd said she was a virgin. Come to think of it, he didn't want her to repeat it. Once had been enough.

Other than a log snapping on the fire, the room was more quiet than he'd ever heard it. Too quiet. He tried to remember some of the things his older brother had said after he'd hurt his wife's feelings. Spence wasn't very good at making amends. Hell, Kane was worse. "Look," he said. "You're young and—" he swallowed "—innocent, but you don't even know me."

"I know I love you."

"You know you—" The blood flow to the lower half of his body came to a screeching halt, right after the blood flow stopped to his brain. It was a good thing Kane had steady instincts. Otherwise he never would have caught the slight hand that was inching dangerously close to certain anatomical parts that would respond no matter what his brain said.

"No, Josie."

Round gray eyes stared into his. "What do you mean no?"

"I mean," he ground out, "I live alone. I work alone. I travel alone. And I'll die alone."

"But you don't have to—"

"Yes, I do." Without another word, he clutched the side of the old claw-foot bathtub with his good hand and pushed to his feet. Water sluiced down his body. Being careful to keep his back to Josie, he reached for a threadbare towel. He felt a little dizzy, but he managed to keep the towel firmly in front of him as he stepped down to the floor.

She was still watching him, still speechless. Wisps of light blond hair had escaped the band on the back of her head, damp tendrils curling over her ears and forehead. She was wearing blue jeans, hiking boots with thick wool socks and a gray-and-blue flannel shirt. He could see the outline of her breasts and the dime-size circle in the center of each of them. Kane had no business noticing, no business responding. And she had no business looking good in that kind of outfit.

Suddenly she moved toward him, her hands reaching around him, drawing the ends of the towel together at his side. Her fingers shook slightly as she tucked the edges underneath. Slowly she raised her gaze to his. "There's plenty of time to think about it, Kane."

Kane was struck speechless all over again. He thought he'd faced the biggest shock of his life when that bullet had sliced through him three days ago. It had been a week of firsts. That had been the first time he hadn't been able to dodge a bullet, and this was the first time anyone had offered him a virgin sacrifice.

"I don't need to think about it, dammit. I already told you I live alone. Besides, you're too young and too skinny."

Josie felt the floor shake as he stomped away. His words might have hurt her feelings, if she hadn't caught a glimpse of—what was it her mama used to say? *The proof is in the pudding.* Whether Kane Slater knew it or not, she'd seen living proof that he didn't find her nearly as repulsive as he claimed.

While he banged around on the other side of the one-room cabin, tugging on his own clean jeans and shrugging into the makeshift sling she'd concocted from one of her brothers' shirts, she drained the bathtub and tidied the place up a little.

He swore loudly and often. Josie let him cuss. His orneriness didn't faze her. Good heavens, she was closely related to five of the grouchiest men on the planet. She'd always wanted a sister, but now she was beginning to think it had been a good thing she'd been exposed to so many grumpy men. She'd been educated by the best. Consequently she shouldn't have too much trouble dealing with Kane's ornery side.

She loved him. She was sure of it now. That made this serious.

She'd thought it would never happen to her. And yet here she was, sitting in a quiet cabin on a quiet mountain, her heart brimming with quiet emotions that simply refused to settle down. She loved a man from Montana, a man who'd risked his life and who claimed he needed no one. No matter what he said, he seemed more lonely than *loner.*

Fishing the soap out of the bottom of the bathtub, she

reminded herself that Kane was very, very stubborn. It just so happened that *she* held the title for that one. A few years ago she'd gone on strike, refusing to cook meals for her brothers and wash their dirty clothes. All because she'd gotten sick and tired of their slovenly ways and lack of manners. At first they'd been downright snide about their refusal to change, but when they were hungry enough and smelly enough, they'd given in. Oh, they were still a little on the slovenly side, but at least now they said "thank you" when she served them their supper and "excuse me" when they belched.

Luckily Kane wasn't slovenly or rude. She was just going to have to find a way to win him over to her way of thinking. Food had been the straw that had broken her brothers' backs. Remembering the way Kane had kissed her and what that kiss had done to *his* body set off a new round of flutters deep in her belly. Something told her that in order to win Kane over, she was going to have to whet his appetite. Not necessarily for food.

She hummed to herself while she added a log to the fire. By the time she'd added carrots and celery to the venison roast she was cooking in the oven, she had broken out in song. Casting a surreptitious glance at Kane, her tune trailed away. He was stretched out on the bed, one leg dangling over the side. Evidently he hadn't been able to manage the shirt on his own. He'd given up, an arm in one sleeve, his other shoulder and arm bare. Eyes closed, he looked pale, his chest rising and falling evenly.

Pressing one hand over her mouth and the other over her heart, she thought, He's beautiful in repose. Striding closer, she imagined herself watching him sleep thirty years from now, thinking the same thing. Of course, he would be older, his face more lined, his body a little thicker. But his chest would still be as broad, his jaw as square, his lips as enticing. She would have liked the freedom to kiss each of those features.

Someday, she told herself. First she had to get to know him better, to become familiar with the little quirks that made up his personality. She wanted to figure out what it took to make him smile and what was behind the low rumbling sound he made deep in his throat.

Covering him with the quilt, she whispered, "Rest now, Kane. You're going to need all your strength for what I have in store for us."

She glanced around the sparsely furnished room before strolling to the window. Outside, the wind had piled the snow in huge drifts, some of them reaching all the way to the branches on trees. She'd uncovered most of the woodpile and had shoveled a path to the outhouse, but the rest of the area was untouched.

The sky was a vivid blue, the sun glinting off the white surface, causing her to squint. It was almost April, and the sun was already trying to melt the snow. Wondering how much longer she would have before Kane insisted he was strong enough to make it down the mountain, she decided she'd better not waste any time. She would begin winning him over as soon as he woke up from his nap.

"I've never even seen Graceland. Can you believe that? Opryland, either, for that matter." Head tipped over, Josie smoothed the brush over her damp hair with long, slow strokes. She couldn't see much beyond the square of floor directly in front of her. Therefore, she couldn't tell if Kane was listening to her or not. It wouldn't be the first time she'd found herself talking to herself when she'd thought she was talking to him. Resigning herself to the possibility, she said, "I guess there are a lot of things I haven't seen in this great big old world."

"You should try to get out of the house once in a while."

She felt her eyebrows go up. "Get out of the house," she repeated, encouraged by his attention. "I get out of the house every day. I just don't get very far in my travels. A storytelling festival takes place in Jonesboro every October. J.D. and Billy tried to get me to go there to spin my tales one year."

"You didn't go?"

"Nah. I'd rather talk to folks I know. I mosey on up to Picket Pass to talk to Nellie Peters every morning after breakfast. Minerva Jones says she can set her clock by me. That woman really appreciates punctuality...."

Kane shifted in the hard-back chair, trying to get comfortable and trying not to notice the way Josie's hair swished with every stroke of her brush. Two days had passed since she'd made her suggestion regarding the method of repayment for all her help. Although she'd talked about everything else under the sun, she hadn't mentioned her, er, virginity again. He squirmed, scowling, because he'd thought about it a hundred times. Her hair crackled; his fingers flexed, his imagination picturing those silken tresses gliding over his skin.

He jerked to his feet.

Jerking to his feet wasn't wise with a sore shoulder. The pain was his own stinking fault. Actually the pain was the fault of the bail jumper who'd shot him. Okay, then the desire shooting through him was his own fault. He knew exactly what to do about it. As soon as he was miles and miles away from here, he'd find a warm and willing woman.

There was a warm, willing woman in this very room.

He swung around fast, swearing out loud at the new shooting pain. Josie was so busy talking she hadn't heard.

"...If I'm not careful I'll end up like Edwina Gilson..."

Talking. Talking. Josie was always talking. She talked while she fixed meals. She'd even talked while she took her bath a little while ago. Kane had kept his back to her the whole time, commending himself on his willpower. Still, every splash had been sheer torture. He was getting worked up all over again just thinking about it. For crying out loud, he didn't even like skinny women.

"…She's seventy-three, and she's never set foot off this mountain."

Pacing to the bed, he reached for what was left of his sheepskin coat and groused, "You call this a mountain?"

Josie went perfectly still. In her efforts to win Kane over, she'd tried being nice. Kane Slater was not an easy man to be nice to. He wasn't an easy man, period. She'd just about used up the last of her patience.

With a toss of her head that sent her hair cascading down her back and around her shoulders, she planted her hands, hairbrush and all, on her hips, and glared at him. "I'm sick and darn tired of all your disparaging comments about my mountain. I don't know what you have against the Blue Ridge Mountains, but they are so mountains. It says so in the encyclopedia. And there's nothing wrong with Tennessee, either. Why, Davy Crockett grew up here, and three United States presidents lived in Tennessee. Don't 'spose you know which ones."

Feeling her blood pressure starting to climb, she took a step toward him. "James Polk and the two Andrews—Jackson and Johnson. I've never seen the mountains in Montana, but if they're anywhere near as big as the chip on your shoulder, they must be huge."

She stared at him across the ensuing silence. Nostrils flaring, he glared back at her, and then, out of the blue, he turned his back on her. She did *not* understand him. Worse, she simply couldn't seem to get a handle on what made him tick. He never reacted to the same situation the same way twice. He yelled, swore or withdrew, in no particular order.

Crossing her arms, she sighed. "What makes the mountains in Montana so special, Kane?"

Kane felt a jolt run through him, yet his feet seemed to be frozen to the floor. Staring at the rough-sawn walls and the bed and the age-old cupboard nearby, he found himself saying, "It's not just the mountains. It's the sky and the air and the way the land stretches toward the horizon as far as the eye can see. Some mornings, it's quiet enough to hear the break of day."

He hadn't been aware that he'd turned around until he saw her lips part and her chest rise with the deep breath she took. She smiled, and his body reacted all over again. In a voice gone soft and gentle, she said, "Quietude isn't something people around me get a lot of."

It took him a full five seconds to drag his gaze away from her smile, but it was the desire thrumming through him that finally brought him to his senses. Heart pounding, he jerked around and tried to put on his coat.

She was there all of a sudden, reaching out with a helping hand, tsk, tsk, tsking about his language. She smelled like shampoo and soap and woman. Placing an iron grip on his resolve, he moved out of her reach. "I can do it myself."

Josie watched him struggle to get the coat over his sore shoulder. He reminded her of a raccoon she'd come across years ago during one of her treks up to Witches Peak. The animal had been stuck in a trap fifteen feet off the beaten path. He was in agony, and would have chewed his own leg off in order to be free, and yet he'd snapped and snarled every time she'd tried to get close enough to help. She'd ended up covering him with her thick coat until she'd managed to open the trap. Free, he'd growled at her until he'd disappeared into the bushes.

Turning on her heel, she strode to the corner where she kept her father's twelve-gauge, thinking, Some creatures simply didn't have it in them to be appreciative.

"What are you doing?"

Gun in hand, she glanced at Kane, who was watching her, obviously unnerved and uncertain of what she was going to do. She pulled a face and sputtered, "I've spent the last five days nursing you back to health. I've put up with your cussing and your grumbling and your ornery tendencies. Do you really think I'd shoot you now? Not that you don't deserve it."

Kane glanced from the long barreled shotgun in Josie's hand to the anger flashing in her eyes. "Then what are you going to do with that gun?"

He heard her loud sigh all the way from the other side of the room. "I brought enough food with me to last me three weeks, at least, but I wasn't expecting company. For an injured man, you eat like a horse."

Trusty shotgun in hand, she stomped out into the snow to try to rustle up something to eat for supper.

Josie dropped a handful of baby onions into the pot then leaned over to add wood to the fire. She might have closed the door with a little more force than was necessary, but she couldn't help it. She considered herself a reasonable woman, but she was close to reaching the end of her rope. She'd spent two and a half hours outside. A person would think all the energy she'd exerted trudging through snowdrifts would have alleviated her anger a little.

Very little.

She'd done a lot of walking and she'd done a lot of thinking, which had led to a lot of soul-searching. She didn't question her feelings for Kane. She questioned her good sense. Adding potatoes and carrots to the bubbling stew, she muttered under her breath. "I've tried everything I could think of to bring out that man's gentler side and what does he do? Practically accuses me of wantin' to shoot him. Why, if I wanted to shoot him I woulda done it by now. If he wasn't so thickheaded and stubborn he'd know that all I want is to get to know him. I've tried being nice. The nicer I am, the grouchier he gets."

She was still sputtering an hour later. Huffing, she reminded herself that she didn't have to take this kind of abuse. Not from her father and brothers. Not from the man she'd been stupid enough to fall in love with. Until he gave her a sign, she was done being nice to him. That decided, she carried two chipped bowls and mismatched cups to the table.

On the other side of the room, Kane grimaced and ducked his head slightly. Amazed that neither of the shallow bowls had broken beneath the force with which Josie had clanked them onto the worn wooden table, he measured her with a long, appraising look.

She'd stomped the snow off her boots and had come inside almost two hours ago. Although she hadn't said a word to him, she'd talked to herself pretty much nonstop. She was wearing another flannel shirt, this one yellow and green. Instead of buttoning it, she'd left it open, revealing a plain white shirt that clung to her thin body.

Ambling closer, he said, "My mother used to sputter like that under her breath, too. I'd forgotten until now."

She looked at him over her shoulder. "Something tells me you gave your mother a lot to sputter about."

Kane shrugged his good shoulder. "What's for supper?"

She waited a good, long time before answering. "Rabbit stew."

Kane strode a little closer. Stomach rumbling, he sniffed the air. She'd been gone two hours before he'd heard the first shot. The second shot had come from someplace closer half an hour later. He'd tried not to watch the clock, he'd tried to sleep and he'd tried to tell himself that the reason he couldn't seem to do either had nothing to do with a guilty conscience.

Kane Slater may have been a lot of things, but he was no liar. He'd screwed up, plain and simple. He'd been ornery, mean and inconsiderate. She'd nursed him back to health, sharing her warm cabin and her food. And what had he done? Treated her unkindly.

"I'm sorry, Josie."

Josie turned around slowly. Kane was looking at her, one arm cradled in the makeshift sling, the other hanging limply at his side. He seemed as surprised by his apology as she was.

"I should have thought. I should have realized. And I should have thanked you," he said, hesitating as if he'd had to dredge the words from a place deep inside him.

She tried to hold a grudge, really she did, but she didn't have it in her to stay angry at this man. She'd hoped he had a gentle side. Like the tip of an iceberg, she was glimpsing it now.

"I know it's no excuse," he said. "But I'm not used to all this inactivity. Sitting around is driving me crazy."

She studied him thoughtfully for several seconds. He'd had another bath that morning, but this time he'd insisted upon doing everything himself. The nick in his chin was the result of shaving with his left hand. Other than that, he'd managed quite well. His light brown hair was clean, the color of his skin more healthy looking. He'd come to her injured and bleeding. The flicker of emotion way in the back of his eyes made her think that his shoulder hadn't been his most serious wound. The realization was dredged from a place beyond logic and reason, a place where there were only shimmery emotions and yearnings older than time.

He'd told her, in no uncertain terms, that he didn't want or need anybody. Need was a funny thing. It could hide deep inside a person, going undetected for years, until one day you noticed it squeezing into your thoughts, into your sighs, into your soul. Kane might not have realized it yet, but he needed a woman's softness, a woman's gentleness, a woman's strength. Not just any woman's. He needed hers.

Going back to her stew, she said, "Apology accepted. And you're welcome. Now, I hope this stew gets done soon. There's nothing like trailing a potential supper for hours to give me an appetite."

She handed him the silverware and told him to make himself useful. She noticed he set the table restaurant style, the fork on the left, spoon and knife on the right. Somebody had taught him manners. Feeling suddenly buoyant, she smiled and said, "It was beautiful out there today. I don't understand what you don't like about the Blue Ridge Mountains. They're just so pretty. Did you know that on a clear day you can see seven states from Lookout Mountain?"

Kane shook his head and lowered onto a straight-back chair. Barely taking enough time to draw a deep breath, Josie continued. "Tennessee is called the big bend state. Wanna know why?"

Kane shrugged. Sure, why not? He was getting used to listening to her stories.

"Because," she said, her long wooden spoon sending steam wafting from the pot of bubbling stew. "The Tennessee River bends in the middle and flows through the state twice. Bubba Jones told me that in the third grade.

He went to Texas to be a rodeo champion. He couldn't hit a bull in the butt with a bass fiddle, let alone ride one, but he ended up marrying a rich widow from Portland, Oregon way. Strange how some things work out, isn't it?''

Kane stared across the small room. He felt dizzy. That happened a lot when he tried to make sense of what Josie said.

She talked on, telling him about people he'd never heard of and places he never planned to go. He glanced up in surprise when she placed the pot of stew on the table and began ladling a healthy portion into his bowl. Breathing in the mouthwatering aroma, he said, "I can't believe there are still women alive who can shoot supper, clean it, dress it, cook it and still have the stomach to eat it after all that."

She dropped onto a chair opposite him and scooped up a spoonful of stew. "It's given me a good understanding of why some people become vegetarians. They say they can't eat the flesh of living creatures. Plants were alive, too, once. How do we know they don't have feelings? I once read that there's an entire segment of our population that talks to their roses and tomatoes and whatnot. I think the human race has to eat something, don't you?"

Kane stared across the table, spoon poised in midair.

"What?" she asked.

"Oh," he said, lowering his spoon to his bowl, "I was just thinking that you're really nothing like I expected a mountain woman to be."

"And how's that?"

Waiting to answer until after he'd taken his first bite of supper, he said, "Bear in mind that what little knowledge I have of mountain people is based on *Beverly Hillbillies* reruns."

"I'm definitely no Granny, and I'm afraid I'm not built like Elly May."

"You don't wear a bra." He clamped his mouth shut. Where had that come from?

Her smile set his teeth on edge. "There's something to be said for small breasts, isn't there?"

He groaned inwardly, his gaze straying below her shoulders. There was something to be said for *her* small breasts. Dragging his gaze away from the gentle slopes evident through the white fabric of her shirt, he cleared his throat and took another bite of stew. He tried not to think about kissing her taut nipples, tried not to wonder if he would be the first.

It was lucky for him that she didn't seem to mind keeping up a one-sided conversation. Funny, a few days ago he hadn't thought there was anything lucky about it. A few days ago he hadn't felt a surging desire when he least expected it. A few days ago he hadn't eaten two bowls of rabbit stew without tasting any of it.

She didn't look at him again until her bowl was empty. Only then did her gaze meet his from the other side of the table. She smiled, and he felt as if the wind had been knocked out of him. He did his best to return her grin, but it wasn't easy, when what he wanted to do was vault over the table and kiss her the way he had the other day in the bath.

"Had enough?" she asked.

Enough? Oh, enough stew. "Yes. Plenty. Thanks."

"Then we'd better get to it."

He gulped. "It?"

"You said you're going stir-crazy. The activity will be good for you."

Activity? Something intense flared through him, something he wasn't certain he'd ever felt in exactly this way. It was the knowledge that she was a virgin. It messed with a man's head, making him think about the darnedest things.

It took the simplicity out of a man wanting a woman. And
Kane believed in keeping things simple.

"Come on, Kane, let's dance."

"Dance? That's what you want to do...dance?"

"What did you think?"

Since Kane wasn't about to admit what he'd been thinking, he said, "There's no music."

She started to hum. Seconds later she broke out into
song. Lord, there she went with the singing again.

"Come on, Kane," she said, drawing him with her to
the center of the room.

"I can't dance," he said, stalling.

Totally undeterred, she placed his good hand on her
shoulder and his other one on her waist, talking all the
while. "I've watched every Fred Astaire and Ginger Rogers
movie ever made a hundred times. I can teach even a mule
with four left feet to dance."

She hummed a few bars of the "Tennessee Waltz."

"Josie, I don't think this is a good idea."

"Don't worry," she whispered, inching closer. "I'll be
real careful of your bad shoulder. There, how's that?"

She started humming again, swaying slightly, easing him
into his first step. "Dancin' ain't—isn't—hard. It's like
playing leapfrog or making love."

He swallowed, his feet moving him around the room, her
voice sending his thoughts to the other side of the moon.
"It's all about trust and consent, about swaying this way
and dipping that way. You hold me just so. And I hold you
just so. There. Feel that?"

Kane felt that, all right. He felt her breasts against his
chest and her hair under his chin. He felt her breath on his
neck and her thighs between his. He felt a lot more than
he cared to admit. It left him warm and wanting, and he
didn't want to stop.

Deciding for once it might be best to keep her talking, he said, "Would you tell me something, Josie?"

She looked up at him and nodded, continuing to hum.

"I was just wondering why a girl who can sing like a lark and glide around the room on feet that don't even touch the ground has stayed on this *mountain*," he said, pausing for quiet emphasis. He really was trying to be nice. "I mean, why would a girl like you stay if you aren't happy here?"

She stared into his eyes for a moment, and then past him as if she was seeing something in the distance only she could see. He watched her expression, intrigued.

"What makes you think I'm not happy here?" she asked.

"Are you?"

She shrugged. "I'm not *unhappy,* if that's what you mean. Some kids don't like school, but I loved it, especially geography and reading. My mama couldn't read very well, but she was so proud of me. I used to talk to her for hours about the people and places I read about and how I was going to visit each and every corner of the world."

"Why haven't you?" he said quietly.

She lifted her chin, her eyes finding his. Their feet continued to move, but their steps took them in a circle that grew smaller and smaller. Taking a deep breath, she said, "Mama got sick when I was fourteen. I missed a lot of school after that. By the time she died, I was seventeen, and Daddy didn't see much sense in sending me back."

Kane had the feeling that for once, Josie was leaving a lot out. A lot of pain. A lot of sadness. A lot of hopelessness. A ton of disappointment. "It's never too late," he said.

"To go back to school? Maybe not in other parts of the country, but in Hawk Hollow, it's way too late. That's why I was hoping to convince you to take me to Montana with you. I'd try to be quiet, Kane. I'm a good cook and a fair to middling housekeeper. And don't all men need a woman every now and then?''

Kane's feet froze to the floor, his hand tightening at her waist.

''Kane?''

There was something in her voice that struck a chord in his heart. Until that instant, he didn't know he still had a heart.

All he had to do was make the next move, and he would find relief for the pent-up need wreaking havoc with his senses. He thought about it. God, it was torture, but he couldn't do it. It seemed that along with a heart came a conscience.

Ending the little dance lesson, he touched her cheek first, and then he straightened her collar. ''I'm tempted, Josie. Believe me, I'm tempted. But a girl like you can do a lot better than a man like me.''

''You're wrong about that, Kane.''

He shook his head, thinking about Obadiah Olson and his tooth. ''Maybe not here, but somewhere. You should do whatever you want to do and be whatever you want to be.''

He hoped he hadn't hurt her feelings too much, and prepared himself for her tongue-lashing and tirade. Neither came. She simply stared at him for several seconds before turning away. He wasn't entirely comfortable with her silence, but the sparkle in her eyes made him downright suspicious.

Chapter Three

That sparkle was still in Josie's eyes three days later. And Kane was still suspicious. He'd been practicing the fine art of holding the opposite sex at bay for years. Women in general didn't make it easy. Josie was more difficult than most.

Now that he was stronger, he'd put a stop to her offers to lend a helping hand. He bathed himself, dressed himself, even took his turn cleaning up after breakfast, lunch and supper. There had been no more dance lessons, no more *anything* lessons. Every once in a while he'd detected what he'd thought was a waning on her part. He was pretty sure she'd given up completely when he'd turned down her far-from-innocent ploy to play strip poker earlier that morning. Now, she seemed more intent upon asking questions than luring him into bed. It was a hard call, but when push came to shove, Kane believed it was far easier to answer her questions than deter her amorous overtures.

"I don't get it," she said, studying the checkerboard between them. "If you want to catch bad guys, why not become a police officer? King me."

Kane turned her checker over dazedly. Studying his next move, he said, "In this age of attorneys and individual rights, police officers' hands are tied. Besides, police departments don't have the time or the resources to chase missing suspects down."

"By resources, you mean money," she said.

At his nod, she asked, "How much does it cost to capture one of these fugitives?"

Kane lifted his gaze from the board, only to find Josie's eyes down-turned. "The average fee for taking a fugitive off the street is five hundred dollars. High profile cases can net anywhere from ten to eighty thousand dollars for an arrest. Those are my specialty."

She shrugged as if thoroughly unimpressed. "Is that why you do it? For the money?"

He shook his head. "I do it because somebody has to. And because I'm good at it. I have a good head on my shoulders and I've learned how a wanted fugitive thinks."

"Have you ever killed anybody?"

That was a question a lot of people asked. Sliding his black checker to the next square, he shook his head. "In the old days a bounty hunter would track and corner his prey. More often than not the confrontation ended in gunfire. It's much safer today."

The sweeping glance she gave the hole in his shoulder spoke volumes.

"This is a first," he insisted.

"Then most fugitives don't mind the idea of going back to jail?"

He shrugged. Most fugitives minded a great deal. That was why most bounty hunters carried a 9mm Beretta and wore bulletproof vests. Kane found vests too heavy and cumbersome, preferring to rely on cunningness and sharp intuition. He didn't see much sense in telling Josie that, so he said, "Being good with a Smith & Wesson helps, but having a strong intuition and steady instincts contribute more directly to the bottom line."

Kane saw his next move as plain as day, and deftly reached for his checker. Josie had the top three buttons on her flannel shirt unfastened before he'd finished jumping her game piece. She was opening the bottom button when he came to his senses.

"You're losing on purpose!"

How she ever managed to turn a simple game of checkers into strip-checkers was beyond him. "I never agreed to do this your way!"

Her shirt fell open, revealing a creamy patch of skin all the way down the center of her torso. Kane's eyes trailed along the delicate ridges of her ribs, getting stuck along the inner swells of her breasts.

"Hold it right there."

"Here?" she asked.

He sucked in a quick breath, thinking he'd better rephrase the statement. "I mean it, Josie. Before you take off that shirt, there's something I want to know. And I expect an honest answer, dammit."

When his gaze finally found its way to her face, he almost forgot what he was going to say. Her eyelashes slipped down then came up again, her gray eyes tender and serene. Calling on the same instincts that had resulted in a healthy bank balance for him and a loss of freedom for wanted fugitives, he said, "Are you throwing the game, Josie?"

The not quite innocent look she gave him before her gaze trailed down his torso could have been the result of a valiant effort gone bad. Or it could have been good acting. He wasn't sure which, but he wasn't going to move a muscle until she answered.

She finally shrugged and said, "Have you ever tried concentrating when a naked man, whom you happen to be in love with, is sitting across the table within touching distance?"

Kane jerked to his feet. "I told you before. You couldn't possibly love me." Glancing down, he scowled. "And I'm only half-naked, dammit."

He'd lost his boots and socks, one at a time. After that, he'd shed two different shirts, his belt, even his sling. One more turn and he would have been down to his skivvies. Naked, he wouldn't have stood a chance.

Josie tried to keep her eyes averted as Kane banged around the cabin. Opening the woodstove door, she added two logs. For lack of anything better to do, she added another. At this rate she was going to roast them right out of the cabin.

Kane was already roasting mad. She could tell by the way he tramped from one end of the room to the other. There was a lot of cussing going on, and an occasional thump and thud. When she finally turned to look at him, he was fully clothed and was pulling on his bloodstained coat, which was more like a vest on one side where she'd cut him out of it.

"What are you doing?" she asked.

His eyes narrowed, but he didn't look at her. "I'm getting out of here."

She couldn't control her panic. "What do you mean?"

"I need some fresh air. Some exercise. Some space."

He picked up the ax that had been leaning near the door and stomped outside. Josie released the breath she'd been holding. He wasn't leaving. He was only going outdoors to take his frustration out on a pile of wood. She didn't see how he was going to do that with his right arm in a sling, but the fact that he was willing to try proved that he was getting stronger every day. Maybe he wasn't leaving the mountain this instant, but he would soon.

Josie was running out of time. It was as plain as the nose on her face. Now that she thought about it, she was a little surprised he hadn't suggested leaving before now. It was only a matter of time. He would leave, and she would be left behind, pining after a man who would never come back for her.

She walked over to the hand pump and filled four of her biggest kettles. After hefting them onto the stove, she looked around the cluttered room. Kane's bed was rumpled, dishes were out, the checkerboard still sitting in the middle of the old pine table. There was plenty to do to keep busy, plenty of time to think about everything she'd tried.

Seducing Kane hadn't worked. Bathing him hadn't worked. Teaching him to dance hadn't worked. Playing strip-checkers with him had been as big a failure as anything. If he would have accepted her offer and had taken her to bed, he would have been her first lover. But her efforts to lure him there hadn't worked, either. He wasn't the first man she didn't understand, and she doubted he would be the last, but he *was* the first man she couldn't handle. He was the only man she'd ever loved.

Although her father said good preachers probably existed, he'd never had much use for the Bible-thumping preacher in Hawk Hollow who ranted and raved about evil sinners who would burn in hell lest they repented and put their money on the collection plate. Consequently what Josie knew about right and wrong came from her heart and the Bible her daddy read from every Sunday morning.

The Bible said love thy neighbor, try not to judge and

forgive those who hurt you. There were a lot of other messages in there, but those were the three Josie lived by.

The water on the stove started to boil. Wrapping a towel around the handle, she carried the kettles, one by one, across the room.

She loved Kane. She didn't understand him, but she supposed he had reasons for wanting to see the last of her. Watching him go was going to be the hardest thing she'd ever done. She stripped out of her clothes and stepped into the bathtub. The warm water brought little relief to her saddened heart.

Kane kept the ax poised over his shoulder for a moment. With a jerk of his elbow, he brought the ax down with a *whack,* the sound echoing through the snow-covered meadow. The log cracked wide open. He swore he knew how that log felt. Although he tried to keep his right arm perfectly still, even the slightest jar reminded him of all the healing he still had in store.

The exercise felt good despite the pain, the view of sun-dappled rocks and snowy pine trees even better. He'd been going stir-crazy, that was all. Or maybe he was going plain crazy. It was Josie. It was being cooped up with Josie eight days in a row. The only time she wasn't talking was when she was singing. He'd tried asking her to please shut up. She'd only smiled, touching her fingertips to his face. That touch had made him want things he had no business wanting. She was eleven years younger than he was and a hundred years more innocent. He wasn't sure what got to him more—her age or her innocence.

Her innocence.

Damn. Things would have been easier if she never would have told him she was a virgin. Of course, he probably would have slept with her by now. And then she wouldn't still be a virgin in the first place. He didn't know how she'd managed to stay a virgin for this long. Fleetingly he wondered why she'd saved herself, and why she'd chosen *him* to be her first lover. No matter what she said, he didn't believe she was really in love with him. She might have been in love with the thought of being in love, but that was all. For crying out loud, she'd only known him for eight days.

He'd been half-dead eight days ago, and unconscious for the next two. For the past six days his body had been letting him know that it was far from dead. It was letting him know right now. Scowling, he brought the ax down on another log.

As a member of the Bail Enforcement Association, Kane had a strict code of ethics. Renegades and rogues didn't stay around long in the bounty-hunting business. He never used excessive force. Those who did turned his stomach. He treated suspects with dignity unless they gave him a reason not to. He used a similar code of ethics in his personal life. He supposed he understood why women gave him a second look. They probably had the same carnal needs as men. But he steered clear of clingy, needy women, and he made it a point not to go near the innocent ones. Their hearts were too big, their bodies too delicate, their feelings too fragile.

That was the problem with Josie. She'd taken him in and laid her heart wide-open, all at once. He could have been a deranged murderer for all she knew, and yet she'd treated him with respect and tenderness, humoring him, tending to his needs, kissing him. He swallowed as he thought about how soft her mouth had felt, and how pliant she'd been, dancing in his arms, and how winsome and graceful she would be in bed.

He clamped his mouth shut and brought the ax down on

another log. He didn't bother swearing at the pain in his shoulder. The pain was better than unspent desire.

He had to get off this mountain. And he had to do it soon. He would tell her after he'd relieved a little more stress. Another ten minutes should do it.

Lowering the ax, Kane eyed all the wood, bark and splinters laying in a heap at his feet. He swiped at a bead of sweat running down the side of his face and heaved a huge sigh. It had taken longer than he'd expected, but he was finally bone-tired and clearheaded. Certain he could keep his hormones in check and his willpower at its highest operating level, he balanced the ax on his shoulder and headed for the cabin.

He opened the door and stepped inside, his eyes squinting as they tried to adjust to the dim interior. He picked up the soft sound of Josie's hum, his eyes peering into the shadows across the room. His first glimpse of her in the clawfoot bathtub stopped him in his tracks.

The humming trailed away. Water splashed. Kane's ax hit the floor with a loud thud. Or maybe that was his heart jump-starting.

For a moment, Josie froze in surprise. Shivering, she called, "Kane, honey, close the door."

He did as she said, then turned toward her once again as if in slow motion. Her thoughts had been so deep she'd lost track of how long she'd been in the bath. Now, the water was lukewarm and the logs in the stove were half gone. And yet she didn't feel cold.

She didn't know what to do, what to say, but she couldn't take her eyes off Kane. His eyebrows were the same color as his hair, the whisker stubble on his chin slightly lighter. She couldn't see the color of his eyes beneath his squint, but she could see the way his features were chiseled, his expression still and serious. He wasn't smiling—far from it—his lips were set in a straight, taut line. His shoulders were taut, too, his fingers curled into fists. His feet were planted, his stance wide, as if he was ready for battle. As one second followed another, she knew what battle he was fighting. Desire, strong and fluid, was setting him on fire.

For a long moment, that burning desire held her still. She had no experience with a man's desire, no knowledge of what she should do with such a fire. Although she couldn't manage even the most tremulous of smiles, she wet her lips. Letting her instincts guide her, she slowly stood.

Kane sucked in a ragged breath as water sluiced down Josie's body. God, she was slight, her shoulders narrow, her breasts puckered as if waiting for his touch. She stepped out of the tub, as winsome and graceful as he'd imagined a little while ago, only to stand before him, shivering and uncertain, and yet quite possibly the bravest *woman* he'd ever known.

That was no girl standing on the other side of the room. She was a woman who happened to be a virgin. Damn. An hour and a half worth of cutting wood, wasted.

There was no disguising his body's reaction to the sight of Josie McCoy, naked and wet. There was no sense pretending that he didn't know what he had to do.

He strode toward her, stopping at the edge of the water puddling at her feet. He reached for a threadbare towel, fully intending to get her wrapped in it before giving her a piece of his mind. But she raised her gray eyes to his, and he couldn't move. He hadn't noticed the curl of her light brown lashes before, or the spattering of freckles across her pert little nose. She was pale, her skin, her eyes, her hair, even her aureoles were pale pink. As the towel fell to the floor, Kane faced the fact that what he wanted to give her was in no way connected to his mind.

He retrieved the towel, his eyes getting caught here and there in the process, his breath getting stuck somewhere between his throat and his lungs. He had every intention of wrapping her in the towel. Instead he smoothed it over her shoulder, down her side, across her waist. He felt her stomach muscles flex when he pressed the towel there. When he finally brought it to her breasts, she whimpered.

Kane's heart chugged with so much force he heard a ringing in his ears. She raised up on tiptoe, pressing her lips to his, and he couldn't hear anything at all. Her breast grazed the skin on the back of his right hand where it rested in his sling. He moved his hand slightly, and she whimpered again.

"Josie," he rasped, trying not to kiss her back. "We shouldn't do this."

Her head tipped back, her eyes opening slowly. "We need to do this, Kane. I want to do this. Don't you?"

He felt her slightest movement—on his hand, and someplace far deeper in his body. "I'm no good for you. I've been standing on the outside looking in far too long to be good for anybody."

Josie's heart swelled with so much feeling she didn't know how she was going to be able to contain it all. She imagined Kane hunkered down in a car parked in the shadows on a dark street, watching other people's lit windows. He saw himself as an outsider. Something about the tone of his voice made her think it went beyond what he did for a living.

He needs me, she thought. My heart, my body, my love.

She lifted her hands, placing them one on either side of his face. His whiskers prickled, but his eyes seemed to be clinging to hers. She wanted to tell him that he wasn't on the outside anymore. She wanted him to know that she was going to take him in, make him a part of her life, a part of *her,* and that as long as she lived, he wouldn't be alone again. But she didn't think he was ready to hear it put into so many words just yet. So, instead of telling him, she kissed him again, and again, showing him with her lips and with her hands and with her body that from this moment on, she was forever his, and he, hers.

He wrapped his good arm around her, bringing her hard against him. Oh, my. Her pulse skittered, her senses leaping with excitement, those butterflies in her stomach back in full force. There was something empowering about the hardness in the body pressing against hers, in the strength in his thighs and the possessive way his arm tightened around her back. There was something intoxicating and mind-boggling in the feel of his lips, in the sound of his breathing and in the way her flesh warmed beneath his touch.

So this was how it felt to be consumed by desire. No wonder so many people sang songs about it and wrote books about it. It was amazing, incredible, positively the most wonderful thing she'd ever experienced.

She wound her arms around his neck, drawing herself up, up, reveling in how wonderful a man could feel. His reaction was swift and violent. She reveled in that, as well.

Her heart thumped, a delicious shudder running all the way through her. What she lacked in experience, she made up for with enthusiasm. Relying on instinct, she moved with him, as if on a waltz, until the back of her legs touched the bed.

It was broad daylight outside, but there was little light filtering through the cabin's one and only window. Heat radiated outward from the woodstove, warming the room, warming her and Kane.

Ah, Kane. She kissed him, over and over. When he followed the outline of her lips with his tongue, she had to hold on to him to keep from sliding to the floor. His kiss was heavenly, but she wanted more.

His eyes opened, his gaze boring into hers. Hoping the expression on his face didn't mean he was still fighting his conscience, Josie said a tiny prayer for courage and slowly slid her hand between their bodies, covering the part of him that was hard with need.

He sucked in a ragged breath. And then, as if he couldn't wait another minute, he shrugged out of his coat and tore off his sling and the shirt that belonged to her father. She helped him with his boots and belt, and with the tricky closure on his jeans. The zipper practically opened by itself.

The jeans came off with little trouble. For a man who had limited use of his right hand, he was amazingly adept.

Goodness gracious, he was a handsome man. He wasn't like the boys she'd grown up with, that was for sure. Practically every man in Hawk Hollow wore union suits in the winter and boxers spring, summer and fall. She knew because they hung over clotheslines or bushes or porch railings for days on end. Kane wore briefs. They hugged his hips like a second skin, a thin cover, but not much of a barrier between them.

She climbed onto the bed, staying on her knees. He sat, laying his cheek against her breast so gently it brought tears to her eyes. Then he turned his head, suckling like a baby. Oh, but he was no baby, his lips, his tongue, his teeth doing the most amazing things to her senses.

He drew her around, onto his lap, and he touched her where no man had ever touched her before. Her eyes popped open in surprise, her breath catching in her lungs. He stared into her eyes, and she swore she'd never seen such a look of entrancement on anybody's face.

The dormant sexuality in her body had been awakened the first night he was here. She'd been waiting eight long days to experience this headiness, this amazing craving for a man's touch, for a man's heat and searing need. No, not eight days. She'd been waiting all her life to feel this way. She'd been waiting all her life for Kane.

She figured he was more experienced than she was. Therefore, he would have to teach her what to do. But she wanted to bring him pleasure, too. Relying on instinct and the expression turning his eyes a darker shade of brown, she moved against him. When he growled like a contented bear, she smiled and did it again.

"Josie."

She covered his lips with her fingertips. He took one into his mouth, and she closed her eyes. How did he do that? How did he make every little touch feel like something alive and brand-new?

"You're only twenty-three."

"Hmm," she whispered. "I'm a grown woman."

Yes, Kane thought to himself. She was a grown woman, a strong, pliant, agile, eager grown woman.

"And you're how old, Kane?" she whispered, gliding her hand between their bodies once again.

His head fell back, his eyes closed. "Thirty-four."

"Thirty-four feels mighty good, doesn't it?"

Lord, so did twenty-three. He almost laughed. "Careful, honey, I'm an injured man."

She didn't stop what she was doing. "I'm awfully glad you're alive."

For the first time in a long time, Kane was glad to be alive, too.

"You'll have to tell me if I do something wrong," she whispered against his neck.

He moaned her name. "You're doing fine without any tutoring from me."

"I aim to please. Show me how."

That was it. No pretending, no excuses, no shyness. Just a straightforward honesty that was the essence of the woman herself. "Oh," Kane murmured, laying her down on the bed and drawing the quilt up over both of them. "I'll show you, and I'll be as slow and gentle as I can be."

Josie wrapped her arms around his neck, little tremors starting low in her belly. They were still new enough to fill her with wonder and still amazing enough to make her wish they never had to stop. He rummaged around under the quilt for a minute. She wasn't sure what he was doing, until he pressed himself against her. She swallowed, in awe of her first reaction to the feel of a completely naked man.

"Oh, Kane."

"I know, Josie. I know."

He levered himself on his left elbow. Keeping his weight off her, he kissed her and touched her and showed her where to kiss and touch him in return. She'd thought she would be a little nervous, being that this was her first time and all. She'd heard that it hurt the first time, sometimes a lot, sometimes only a little. She figured the pain couldn't be that bad, or else women would only do it once, and she'd overheard Betsy Crandal whispering to Miriam Orweller about how many times in one week she laid down with her man. Josie had gasped at the number.

She gasped again as pleasure, pure and explosive, sent something a lot bigger than butterfly wings quivering in her belly. The next thing she knew Kane was pressing her legs apart with his knee and positioning himself directly over her. She wasn't afraid. She was too mesmerized by the expression on Kane's face to feel anything except joy.

She heard a whooshing in her head, and what sounded like thunder. Could it be a thunderstorm? An avalanche? The end of the world?

Before she could make sense of the sound of the door

banging open and of the cold air bursting into the room, a loud voice bellowed, "Hold it right there you dirty rotten scoundrel. And take your filthy, no-good, womanizin' hands off my daughter or I'll blow you to smithereens!"

Chapter Four

"I said unhand my daughter. *Now.*"

Daughter?

Kane came to his senses the way lightning found the ground, with a half second of blinding light and a staggering jolt of understanding. If Josie was this man's daughter, the old mountaineer glaring at Kane through the sights of that double-barreled shotgun was Saxon McCoy, and the four younger versions spreading out near the door were her brothers, Billy, James, Roy and J.D.

Kane had been in a lot of tricky situations in his lifetime, but this one was brand-new. He eyed the door, the peg where he'd hung his gun and holster, and finally, Josie. Her eyes were huge, her face tinged with embarrassment. Using his left arm, he levered himself off her. Since he didn't relish the idea of facing the firing squad buck naked, he searched very carefully beneath the blankets for at least one article of clothing.

"Put your hands where I can see 'em," Saxon said in a menacing growl.

Josie raised up on one elbow and peeked at her father over Kane's shoulder. Her initial shock was subsiding, along with her initial embarrassment. "What do you think he has under these sheets, Daddy, a weapon?"

Her father returned her glare. "I know what he has under them sheets, young lady."

Her two middle brothers smirked, their grins sliding away at their father's dark look.

"It's all right, Josie," Kane said. "I'll handle this."

Another time her heart would have swelled with gratitude over the fact that the man she loved had placed himself between her and danger, but right that second she was piping mad about the interruption. "It is not okay. I thought I told you boys I'd come home when I was good and ready. And close the door, James. Were you born in a barn?"

The room was so still Kane swore he heard four triggers being set. "Easy, Josie," he said. "Don't make them mad."

The old man nodded at the son closest to the door. Seconds later, James slammed it shut. "Now," Saxon said, turning back to the bed, his voice as deep and dangerous as any Kane had ever heard. "Who the hell are you?"

Josie's voice wavered from the other side of the narrow mattress. "This is Kane Slater, Daddy. He's a bounty hunter from Montana. He stumbled into this cabin eight days ago, shot and bleeding. I've been nursing him back to health."

"Is that what you call it?" one of the brothers asked.

"Shut up, J.D.," Josie grumbled.

"You shut up."

"I told you first."

"I told you second."

"For crying out loud," Saxon bellowed. "The way the two of you carry on makes it difficult to know whether I should shoot the both of ya or turn the gun on myself. Now shut up while this stranger and I conduct a little business.''

Business? Kane thought to himself. He could hold his own with most men. He wasn't so sure about this one. Saxon McCoy, with his bushy gray hair and long, grizzly white beard, was every bit as scary as his name. It was more than the double-barreled shotgun. The man was huge, his shoulders massive, his chest broad. The brothers, although not quite as grizzly, were no less intimidating.

He glanced at Josie, whose gray eyes were large, and then at the wall where his Beretta was hanging in its holster underneath his bloodstained shirt. The odds were stacked against making a run for it. Since he would prefer not to die in bed, he swung his feet to the floor and stood.

Looking down the wrong end of five shotguns wasn't something he enjoyed. Doing it buck naked made it worse, but at least it was better than trying to talk from the wrong side of the sheets.

There was a rustle behind him. The next thing he knew, Josie, all wrapped up in the quilt, placed herself directly in front of him. ''Have you no manners?'' she admonished her father and brothers. ''Can't you see that Kane needs a little privacy?''

Eyes narrowing to the point of disappearing in his craggy face, the old mountain man moved the barrel of his gun up and down a few times and snorted, ''Me 'n the boys were worried about you. So we decided to trek up here and make sure you were all right.''

Josie's snort was as big as her father's. ''You know dang well I can take care of myself. You're just gettin' tired of doin' your own cooking and washing your own clothes and taking care of your own messes.''

The brother who had closed the door said, ''You ain't hardly in no position to be making us mad.''

"I'm twenty-three years old. I can do anything I want."

"Can not."

"Can so."

"Can not."

She stuck her tongue out at James, who glared at her in return. Saxon intervened. "Put a lid on it, the both of ya. Good God, girl, we're practically starving on our own cookin', but things sure have been peaceful these past few weeks."

"Things will go on being peaceful as soon as you and the boys leave."

Kane didn't wait a moment longer than he had to to step out from behind Josie. Partially dressed in faded jeans, he stared directly into Saxon's eyes. "What Josie said about me is true. I *am* a bounty hunter from Montana. I got shot on a ridge several miles from here. It was lucky for me I stumbled upon this cabin. Josie's been taking care of me."

Saxon snorted.

Kane fought hard not to swallow the nervous lump in his throat. That hadn't come out the way it was supposed to. One of the brothers who hadn't spoken took a step toward his sister. "Looks like you nursed him back to health for nothing, Josie. Want me to shoot him, Daddy?"

"Don't shoot him!" Josie cried.

Saxon lowered his gun, but not his gaze. "Josie, get dressed and wait outside."

Kane heard Josie's gasp. A glance in her direction was all it took to see her eyes glaze with tears. Holding the quilt securely around her, she said, "Daddy, you can't shoot him. I love him."

Her declaration made Kane more uncomfortable than all five cocked shotguns, combined. "Look," he said, "I'm sure Josie doesn't mean that."

One wave of Saxon's gun silenced Kane. "You soiled

my daughter. I aughta shoot you whether she loves you or not.''

"Sir. I can explain.''

"It's a little late for explanations. Just be quiet and le'me think.'' He scratched his craggy beard, eyeing Kane long and hard.

Kane had never planned to grow old. He'd faced death eight days ago. That was the way he'd thought the end would come. Something in this old mountain man's eyes told Kane he wasn't really going to shoot him. It allowed Kane to take a steadying breath. Carefully gauging the other McCoy men's expressions, Kane finally said, "You can see my shoulder is healing. I'd be dead if not for Josie. I have two brothers in Montana I'd really like to see again. I'll leave Tennessee immediately. You'll never see me again. We'll just forget this ever happened.''

Josie's heart lurched. Forget it? How could he forget it? She'd almost made love for the first time. She wanted to finish it, not forget it. "You want to leave me?'' she whispered. "After everything that's happened between us these past eight days, you want to leave and never come back and forget all about me?''

"Ah, Josie girl,'' Saxon mumbled, "Don't cry.''

"I can't help it, and I'm not crying much, Daddy.'' She bit her lip and swiped at her cheeks. She hadn't cried in front of the whole family in years, not since her mother had died and her father told her she couldn't go back to school.

Josie met her father's stare. He had that look on his face again, the one he always wore when he didn't know what to do or say to his only daughter. She sighed, and lowered her gaze to the floor.

After a moment of silence, Saxon said, "Kane Slater? Is that what Josie said your name is?''

At Kane's nod, the old man continued. "I'd say the worst punishment I could wish on you is that you have a daughter like Josie someday. Course, a girl like her would be your biggest reward, too. I don't care what anybody says. Raising girls ain't like raising boys. It isn't that you love them more. You just love them different. What would you do, Slater, if you walked in on your daughter in a situation like this someday?"

Josie glanced at her brothers, who were shifting uncomfortably from one foot to the other. Holding the quilt firmly under her arms, she looked at Kane. Head held high, he met her father's steady gaze. An unexpected warmth surged through her. After all these years, she'd finally met a man who was equal to her daddy.

"Well?" Saxon prodded. "You gonna answer?"

"I'd probably want to shoot him, too," Kane said quietly. "Since I'm never going to have children, I guess I'll never know for sure."

"A war injury?" Saxon asked.

A look of consternation crossed Kane's face, followed closely by a look of understanding and a slow shake of his head.

"Have a bad case of the mumps when you were younger?" one of her brothers called from the back of the room.

She saw Kane's shoulders rise, his chest puff up. "I didn't say I *couldn't* father children. I'm just not planning to."

"Why the hell not?" Saxon sputtered.

Yeah, Josie thought. Why the hell—heck—not?

Kane's chin came up a fraction of an inch. "I have my reasons. They're personal."

He chose that moment to look at her, his gaze meeting

hers for one fleeting second. There it was again. The lonely look of a man standing outside, looking in.

It wasn't easy for Josie to smile, when what she wanted to do was place her hand in his and kiss him in front of her father and brothers and her mother if she was watching from heaven, but smile, she did. Her oldest brother, Billy, whistled between his teeth and said, "Well, I'll be. Looks like our little sister really is all grown-up."

Kane was aware of the change in Saxon. Tension was back in his shoulders, accusation was back in his eyes. "You're gonna have to do right by my daughter."

Every nerve in Kane's body went on alert. "Do right?"

Four shotguns in the back of the room were aimed and pointed once again, but it was the ominous quality in Saxon's voice that caused Kane the biggest concern. "Her reputation's ruined. You've soiled her. You're going to have to marry her."

"Marry her!" Kane had spoken without intending to.

Saxon didn't budge, not even to nod.

"I didn't soil— We didn't— You can't force—" Kane floundered, choked and turned to Josie. "Tell them, Josie. They'll listen to you."

Her eyes were raised to his, the pupils large and black and as full of surprise as he was.

"Josie?"

She lowered her gaze to her toes. For once in her life, she remained utterly silent.

Kane took a quick sharp breath, a sense of disbelief slowly turning into a roaring din in his ears. He took his time looking each of the McCoy brothers in the eye. When he faced the steely expression in Saxon's stare, he knew his fate was sealed. He'd heard that some mountain people still practiced the ways of their ancestors, planting corn and making soap by the signs of the moon, but he could hardly believe shotgun weddings still took place in this day and age.

Unless Saxon changed his mind, Kane was going to have to marry Josie McCoy.

Josie clasped her hands together then turned to study her reflection in the chipped oval mirror. They'd all arrived back in Hawk Hollow an hour ago, her father, her brothers, her and Kane. She'd spent the time getting ready. An hour wasn't very long, but she'd done what she could with her hair, piling it on top of her head and securing it with four pearly white combs. Her hair had always had a mind of its own. It seemed her wedding day was going to be no exception. More tendrils were escaping the combs every minute, wispy blond tresses brushing her eyebrows, skimming her ears and curling down the back of her neck.

"Oh, Mama," she whispered to her own reflection in the mirror. "I wish you were here to tell me I look pretty in this dress and that I'm doing the right thing."

She smoothed her hands down the softly gathered fabric that made up the skirt, wondering if her mother had been nervous when she'd been making this dress to wear on the day she would marry big Saxon McCoy.

Josie turned in a circle, smiling at the thought of her mother's steady hand. The dress was made of the softest brushed cotton Josie had ever worn. It was pale pink and was dotted with hundreds of tiny pink rosebuds. It wasn't the usual type of dress worn at weddings, but then, this wasn't the usual kind of marriage.

The pit of Josie's stomach dipped dangerously low, then threatened to turn upside down. She placed her hand beneath her ribs and took several calming breaths. The woman gazing back at her in the mirror didn't appear any calmer. She looked young and fragile and scared to death.

She hadn't bothered with makeup, but her lips had turned dark pink where she'd chewed on them. She backed up until a patch of weak spring sunlight fell across one side of her face. It turned her eyelashes golden brown, and made her eyes look big and round and almost pretty.

She wondered if Kane would think she was pretty. He'd found her attractive enough to kiss her, and touch her, and lay down with her. Of course, that was probably hormones as much as anything else. Still, she sensed that he was an honorable man, and she didn't believe he would have made love to somebody he didn't like at least a little.

He'd been mighty quiet the first several days they were together, but the last few days he'd started opening up. He'd answered her questions, now and then offering her a shred of insight into his personal life. She'd even caught him smiling once or twice. He hadn't cracked so much as a smirk since the moment her father had told Kane that he was going to have to marry her.

Lord, what was she doing?

She'd heard J.D. come back with Owen Crandal, the justice of the peace, a few minutes ago. As soon as her father came for her, the wedding would begin. If she let it.

"Mama," she whispered to the ceiling. "What am I gonna do?"

Josie jumped when the door opened behind her.

"My, my, my," her father said, striding into her room, tugging at the collar of his one and only dress shirt. "If you don't look pretty, I don't know what does."

"Where's Kane?" she asked in a choked whisper.

"He's waitin' in the living room with your brothers. What's the matter, girl? You're as hop-skippity as a sparrow with a broken wing."

She smoothed her hands down the skirt of her dress only

to wind up wringing them in front of her. "I don't think I can go through with this, Daddy."

"You're nervous about the wrong thing, girl. You should have thought about this before giving up your virginity to a perfect stranger."

Josie narrowed her eyes and brought her chin up. "That's just it. Kane doesn't feel like a stranger."

"Of course he don't, not after you and he—"

"We didn't."

"You mean you—"

She shook her head. "I'm still a virgin. No thanks to you."

"Then he—"

She shook her head.

He scratched his thick beard. "Why didn't you say something?"

She turned away. "Because I love him, and I want to go with him wherever he goes."

"You really want to marry a man who's being forced?"

"No. I want him to want to marry me, too. I think there's a place deep in his heart that needs a woman, that needs me. The thought of never seeing him again makes my heart ache, Daddy. I'm afraid if I marry him, he'll hate me. I'm afraid if I don't marry him, I'll hate myself. It isn't as if he has to *stay* married to me, is it? You're the one always sputtering that nowadays getting a divorce is as easy as buying a loaf of bread. I won't fight him, if it comes to that. If I can't reach the part of his heart that needs me, I'll have to let him go, but if I don't marry him, how will I ever know?"

"Ah, Josie-girl. You really think he needs you?"

At her nod, Saxon blinked his eyes and cleared his throat. "You're just like your mama, do you know that?"

Josie swallowed, too. From Saxon McCoy, that was high praise. "What am I gonna do, Daddy?"

Saxon's cough didn't fool Josie. Clearing his throat again, he said, "I asked your mama the same thing before she died. 'What am I gonna do, Emmaline?' I asked. 'With five young 'uns, three of them not fully raised and all of 'em as wild and sassy as they can be.' Know what she said?"

"What did Mama say, Daddy?"

"She told me to trust my heart first, and my instincts second and that she was glad she married me. She said not to worry, because she'd be watching from above. I took her advice, and I've gotta say it's worked out so far."

Josie's head tipped slightly, her heart swelling with feeling for this big, burly man. "Then that's what you think I should do? Trust my heart and my instincts?"

He nodded. After a long silence, he said, "I'm going to miss you, girl."

She went into his arms, whispering that he was going to miss her cooking.

"That, too," he mumbled hoarsely. "That, too."

Kane gritted his teeth and strode to the window. Other than snow melting off the roof of the house next door, and the roof of the house next door to that one, there wasn't much to see on the other side of the wavy glass. Three of the four McCoy brothers were manning their positions in various locations throughout the small living room. The other one was standing watch on the front porch.

They were much less talkative than their sister, grunting something to one another every now and then. Billy, the oldest, had returned Kane's gun a while ago. Roy, the third brother, had told him he'd return the bullets right after the ceremony, along with the keys to his truck, which had been found over on Witches Peak. Kane had practically choked on a scathing retort. He wanted to demand that they return both now, but he knew it would be useless.

He'd known this was serious by the look in Saxon's eyes up in that cabin. Kane had been a bounty hunter for twelve years and had become adept at thinking on his feet. He'd planned to keep his eyes and ears open during the trek down the mountain. He'd figured he would find the right moment to escape and seize it. They'd walked less than a mile when they'd come across four snowmobiles. Riding behind Roy, there hadn't been a single opportunity to escape.

Plan B had entailed getting a few minutes alone with Josie and talking some sense into her. He hadn't seen more than the back of her head since she'd climbed onto the snowmobile behind her father. Kane hadn't come up with Plan C.

He felt in his pocket for a pack of cigarettes. J.D. must have recognized the gesture because he produced a pack along with a book of matches. "Relax," the youngest McCoy brother said. "You could do a lot worse than our Josie."

Kane scowled. That might have been true if he'd wanted to get married. Which he didn't.

He took several draws on the cigarette, waiting for the nicotine to kick in. He'd paced from a worn old sofa back to the window when James handed him an ashtray. "Josie doesn't like ashes on the floor."

Kane glanced at James, and then at the little boy with flaming red hair who was making a beeline for the oldest McCoy brother. "Daddy," the boy said, holding up his hands.

Billy McCoy scooped the child into one strong arm. The boy, who looked to be two or three, was obviously very comfortable in the big man's arms. He didn't, however, look anything like the rest of the McCoys. Kane couldn't help wondering if the mother had flaming red hair. Now that he thought about it, he couldn't recall hearing Josie mention the boy's mother—a hundred other people, but no sister-in-law. There weren't any signs of her here in this house.

Kane glanced around the room. He'd half expected the place to look like mountain shacks he'd seen on television, complete with a sagging roof, boarded-up windows and walls insulated with newspaper. The McCoy house wasn't large, but it was fairly clean. There was real wallpaper on the walls and threadbare but adequate furniture lining the room. One end table held a frilly doily. The top of the television held a Bible. Some woman had made the house a home. Whether it had been Billy's wife, or Josie, Kane didn't know.

Nor did he care.

He flicked the ashes into the heavy, misshapen tray and resumed pacing. With their "Josie this and Josie that," it was obvious that she was the family favorite. Kane wanted to ring her slender little neck. So what if she'd saved his life. He would have been better off taking his chances in the wild. Dead, but better off.

He stomped to the other side of the room and crammed his cigarette into the bottom of the ashtray. He was restless and irritable. Hell, who wouldn't be? He'd walked into a trap and no amount of pacing was going to get him out of it. He gritted his teeth and clenched his jaw tighter. If Josie McCoy, with her long stringy hair and skinny little body, thought he was going to go peacefully, she could think again. She couldn't make him say I do, and neither could her family. What were they going to do? Shoot him?

Fine. Let them.

He'd already been shot once. It wasn't fun, but it was better than being forced to marry a scrawny little woman he barely knew. If he died, so be it. If he was unconscious, he couldn't very well say I do. What would Josie do then? Cry—her eyes filling with tears, her lips quivering, her face going pale? She wasn't his concern. She could cry until the cows came home. He didn't care. He rued the day he'd laid eyes on her. He wasn't going to marry her, and that was final.

A door opened on the other side of the room. Kane turned around automatically as Josie stepped into the room on Saxon's arm. Kane's hands fell to his sides, his heart chugging to life.

She was slight, and as winsome and graceful as a dancer. Her hair was piled on top of her head; her gray eyes were large and luminous. He'd never seen her in a dress, certainly not a dress like the one she was wearing. The bodice was tight, the neckline low, drawing attention to her breasts, which puckered before his eyes. Kane swallowed. Didn't she know enough to wear a bra on her wedding day?

He gritted his teeth and fought down his desire with everything he had. The justice of the peace took his position at the front of the room. Saxon placed Josie's hand on Kane's arm, nodded once, then took a step back.

The thin, stoop-shouldered man in a moth-eaten suit and horn-rimmed glasses began to read from a small pamphlet in his hand. There was no music, no preliminary prayers, no "Dearly beloved, we are gathered here..." If Kane hadn't known better, he would have thought the man was giving him a speeding ticket. Kane grunted out loud. He should be so lucky.

"Josephine Marie McCoy, do you take this man to be your lawfully wedded husband?"

Kane's eyebrows quirked slightly. *Josephine?* But Josie didn't hesitate to answer, "I do."

"And you, Kane Slater—that is your legal name, isn't it?"

Kane almost told the man that Kane Slater was the name his parents gave him the day he was born, but he made the mistake of shrugging, the pain in his shoulder reminding him of the man who had shot him. Staring straight ahead, he answered, "It's what my enemies call me."

Josie almost gasped. Afraid to look at Kane, she'd been staring straight ahead, but the harsh, raw sound of his voice drew her gaze. She watched him in silence, wondering about his strange reply. She'd known he had enemies. A man didn't wander around in a blizzard with a gunshot wound unless he had at least one. Gazing at his prominent cheekbones, his straight nose and strong chin, she wondered what his friends called him. She wondered if he had friends. The thought of him facing the world alone sent an ache to her heart.

Owen Crandal cleared his throat. "In that case," he said, his nasally voice shaking slightly, "do you, Kane Slater, take this woman to be your lawfully wedded wife?"

Josie held her breath. If Kane said no, she would stop the wedding. She would let him go. And things would go back to the way they used to be. She would still have her father and her brothers and her nephew and her friends on the mountain. But she would have no one to love in that special way, and no one to love her in return. Consequently she would go through the motions of life without really living. She would grow old and brittle without ever really knowing real joy, without ever experiencing anything beyond her ordinary, mundane existence. If Kane said no…

Kane made the mistake of glancing down at Josie. She was looking up at him, her eyes deep and teary. Her lips quivered, her throat convulsing as if on an unuttered wish. He knew how the skin at the base of her neck felt beneath his lips, how pliant and agile she felt beneath his hands. The shock of her ran through his body, making it nearly impossible to tear his gaze away.

Saxon cleared his throat behind him in warning. Kane closed his eyes and shook his head. "Better wed than dead, I suppose."

The McCoy brothers' snickers earned them a glare from Josie, but before she could shake a stick at them, the justice of the peace said, "Is that a yes?"

Kane started to shrug. Glimpsing the barrel of a gun out of the corner of his eye, he ended up saying, "Yes, I guess it is."

"In that case, I now pronounce you husband and wife." The room fell silent.

"Well," Saxon finally said. "I guess that's that."

"I guess that's that," the child said, mimicking his grandfather.

Kane glanced down at the four signatures on the paper he'd signed when he'd first arrived in Hawk Hollow. He didn't know how Owen Crandal had gotten around the usual blood tests and three-day waiting period, but as a bounty hunter, Kane knew enough about the workings of the law to understand that every law had at least one loophole. Obviously there was a loophole in this law big enough to throw a cat through. Rubbing his thumb over the raised seal on the legal document, he thought, yes, it certainly looked as if that was that.

Kane Slater was a married man.

Floorboards creaked beneath Kane's feet as he paced from one end of the McCoy house to the other. Josie's family had left fifteen minutes ago, Saxon looking slightly green around the gills while the brothers grinned. Subtle, they weren't.

Kane glanced sharply around, furious. He'd tried the door earlier. Finding it unlocked, he'd thought about walking through it and never returning. What good would it do him? He would still be a married man. Josie had the piece of paper to prove it. The thought stopped him in his tracks and sent a rush of expletives through his head.

There had to be something he could do. Maybe it wasn't too late to talk some sense into that woman. He stomped into Josie's tiny bedroom just as she was coming out of the bathroom down the hall. She walked as far as the doorway, paused and slowly closed the door.

"Josie," he said. "You know this can never work."

She moved on to pull the shade against the darkness that was gradually seeping into the sky. And then she turned to him. "What can never work, Kane?"

Kane should have known she was trouble the first time he laid eyes on her. The fact that he'd been half-dead was no excuse. He should have turned tail and run instead of passing out on her floor.

"Kane?" she whispered, bending to turn on an old-fashioned lamp next to her bed.

He froze for a moment. Heart pounding, he cast her a withering stare. She didn't wither at all. She wet her lips, letting her hand trail over the threadbare chenille spread covering the thin mattress. Kane's heart knocked against his ribs, and lower, desire sprang to life.

She was still wearing the pink dress with the tiny rosebuds, but her feet were bare, her face clean-scrubbed, her hair tumbling down her back and shoulders. The pupils of her eyes were dilated in the near darkness, so that only a ring of gray encircled them. Holding his gaze, she said,

"There are some kinds of trouble you can't run from, Kane."

What was this? Could she read his mind, too? "I don't like being forced, dammit."

"Give it a try, Kane." She patted the bed. "Give marriage a try."

She laid down on the bed, the pulse at the base of her neck fluttering wildly, the invitation in her eyes as clear as could be. Kane took a quick, sharp breath. Until that very afternoon, it had been a long time since he'd had a woman in his bed. And that afternoon he hadn't finished what he'd started.

He found himself lowering to the edge of the mattress. She raised up on one elbow and kissed him. Not the way she had before, but sweetly, shyly. Hell, he thought, but he didn't pull away.

She took his hand in hers and slowly placed it over her heart. Kane took it from there, gliding it inside the bodice of her dress, covering her breast as his mouth covered hers once again. She made a mewling sound in the back of her throat, cupping his face in her small hand. His skin prickled as passion pulsed through his veins.

A horrendous racket sounded outside the window. Kane jerked his head up, twisting toward the sound.

"Oh, no," Josie said. "They're giving us a belling."

"What the hell is a belling?"

"It's another word for a shivaree. It's a serenade mountain folks give a newly married couple. It's part of the honeymoon ritual. They'll go away in an hour or two. Don't worry."

Kane's hand was still on her breast. He stared at it for a long moment. Coming to his senses, he jerked to his feet and spun around. What in Sam Hill had he gotten himself into? Raising his voice over the racket of horns and cowbells and what sounded like a mandolin, he said, "Pack your things."

"My things?" she asked, slowly rising to her feet.

His nod was sharp and swift. "I've had all the surprises I can stand for one day. We're leaving for Montana immediately."

"But Kane, it's dark out, and you're injured, and it's been a long day."

His eyes darkened dangerously. "Be ready in ten minutes."

She'd heard the unspoken "or else" loud and clear. Without another word, he turned and left the room.

Josie sank onto the mattress, her gaze straying to her reflection in the oval mirror across the room. Twisting the wedding ring that had once belonged to her mother, Josie glanced around the room that had been hers for twenty-three years. In ten minutes, she would be leaving it as a married woman, in name if not in deed.

She jumped to her feet. Kane had given her ten minutes. She'd better get busy, because her new husband would leave without her if she wasn't ready on time.

She reached underneath the bed for her battered old suitcase. Popping it open, she tried to decide what to pack first. After emptying one drawer, she glanced at her watch. She had nine more minutes.

Nine minutes before her life as a married woman truly began.

Chapter Five

It was dark outside the windows of Kane's pickup truck. And quiet. Too quiet. Josie didn't know how much longer she was going to be able to stand Kane's silent treatment, but two could play that game. Even if it killed her.

Kane had given her ten minutes to pack. She'd been ready and waiting in nine. He hadn't said anything when she'd stashed her dilapidated suitcase and box of tools in the back of his truck, and neither had she. She hadn't been able to hear what her father had said to him before Kane had climbed behind the wheel. As far as she could tell, Kane's only response had been one grudging nod. They'd driven away when the last ray of sunshine was barely a blush in the western sky, amidst the noise and racket of cowbells and horns and James on the mandolin.

Since the last thing she'd wanted to do was give Kane a reason to take her home, she'd been careful to hide her sniffles and tears as they'd left her mountain. Besides, she hated being told *"I told you so."* She needn't have worried.

Other than a few mumbled "yeses" and "nos", Kane hadn't said a word all night.

Josie hadn't expected a man like him to be happy with his situation, at least not at first, but she hadn't expected the fury in his expression or the way he kept his teeth clenched, either. She didn't think he'd be able to operate the shifting lever, what with the way his right shoulder was injured and all, but Kane Slater was obviously very inventive, because he shifted with his left hand and steered with his right. Still, she could tell every movement cost him.

After getting her ears singed following her offer to drive, she'd kept quiet. No small feat for Josie McCoy. Josie *Slater,* now. She smiled at the thought. It wasn't the first time a smile had crept across her face. Why, she'd nearly burst with excitement when they'd passed the sign welcoming them to Kentucky. Part of her dream was coming true with every passing mile.

An approaching car lit up the inside of the truck, white light creeping across Kane's face. Studying the chiseled profile of the man she'd married, she had a feeling it was going to take a while for the rest of her dream to come true. That was okay. She was a patient woman. She had the rest of her life to find a way into Kane's heart.

It was hard to tell how long they'd been on the road. The radio said one thing, her watch said another. She'd fallen asleep right about the time the horse farms of Kentucky gave way to the rolling hills of Southern Indiana. The sun was coming up when she opened her eyes the next time. One look at Kane's face and she knew he was on the verge of exhaustion. His face was drawn, his cheeks hollow, his eyes hooded.

"Do you want to get a room somewhere?" she asked.

He shook his head.

"Then say the word when you're ready for me to drive."

His answer was more like a grunt than an actual word, but he slid over on the seat and gave her free rein of the steering wheel. His head had started to bob before she'd pulled out of the rest area.

Glancing at the pallor of his skin and the deep lines beside his mouth, she eased the clutch to the floor and jiggled the shifting lever into second gear. So far so good.

"Now," she whispered to herself, her left hand gripping the steering wheel. "Where in the world is third?"

The grinding sound coming from the transmission was slightly jarring, but it was nothing compared to the way Kane jerked awake, winced, swore and sputtered, "I thought you knew how to drive."

"I do."

"Then for crying out loud, leave a few teeth on third gear, would you?"

"I'm trying," she muttered. "I just haven't driven a stick shift in a while, that's all."

The transition into fourth was slightly better. Sighing in relief, she chanced a glance at Kane. He was glaring at her. "How long has it been since you've driven a stick?"

She shrugged. "Five years, give or take a few months."

"Five years." The truck jerked a few times, making Kane wince and cuss all over again. "And how many times did you drive a stick shift five years ago, give or take a few months?"

She swallowed. "A couple."

"Are you telling me your father and brothers never saw to it that you'd mastered driving a stick shift?"

Making a valiant effort to relax the white-knuckled grip she had on the steering wheel, she said, "Daddy tried. Once."

"Once? What do you mean once?"

"Don't yell at me," she declared. "I'm doing the best I can."

Keeping a safe distance between her and the car in front of her, she tried to decide how much to tell him. Since she preferred being yelled at to being ignored, she said, "The boys all tried to teach me to drive a stick shift, but they don't have a lick of patience between them, so Daddy decided to try his hand at it. He took me out to the old mountain road when I was eighteen. I've got to say that a mountain road ain't—isn't—a good place to try to teach somebody to drive anything, let alone a stick shift. Daddy kept his voice real steady, pointing out the things I needed to know. I listened real hard, honest I did. To this day he swears he told me I had to push in the clutch when I used the brake, but I don't think he mentioned any such thing."

"Pull over."

Bouncing along at an even keel, she continued as if Kane hadn't spoken. "The next thing I knew we were barreling down the curving road, over bumps and ruts and washouts. Who knows where I would have ended up, if it hadn't been for Morris Baxter's moonshine shed. The hole's still in it. I should have shown you before we left Tennessee."

"I said pull over."

"Old Morris was spitting mad, but there wasn't much he could do about it. Daddy told him if he didn't pipe down he was going to call the sheriff himself. The sheriff knew about Morris's moonshining, but a call like that would have forced the sheriff to do something about it. Morris settled down, and Daddy never called, but word travels fast on the mountain. After that, nobody within fifty miles would let me near their standard transmissions."

"Pull over, dammit. Or I'll—"

"Or you'll what?" she asked, glancing at him. "You're tired, and I know your shoulder's paining you. You can't do this on your own, Kane, and you don't have to. I can drive this truck. Honest I can. I'm your wife now. It's okay to need me. We're a team, you and me. You look done in. Why don't you try to go to sleep for a little while? You'll feel a lot better when you wake up. I promise."

Kane glanced at the instrument panel, at the long stretch of highway in front of them and the handful of cars sharing the road. It was eighteen hundred miles from Hawk Hollow, Tennessee, to Butternut, Montana. According to the map, they had thirteen hundred miles to go. It was a hell of a long trek when he was fit and rested. His shoulder ached and his mind was groggy. Josie was right about the fact that he needed to rest. But what she'd said about him needing her wasn't true. He needed no one. She may have finagled a way to force him to marry her, but she couldn't force him to like it. And they sure as hell weren't a team. One of these days, he would find a way to convince her of that. Laying his head against the window, he thought about telling her right now. But Josie was talking, and his eyes closed. He would tell her later.

"His name was Beavis. And here everybody thinks the man who created the cartoon made that name up," Josie laughed. "Anyway, Beavis and his wife, Annabell, were on their way to Graceland when Annabell spotted a man she swears was Elvis. I never thought much about it, but the way she described him, why, it even made Daddy wonder if Elvis might still be alive. Anyway, Beavis and Annabell had been combing the mountains looking for him. I thought they were a little strange, but Daddy let them stay one night. Mountain folks are hospitable, if not entirely trusting."

Kane opened one eye at a time. Eyeing the plain gold ring on Josie's finger, he thought *no kidding*. He glanced out the window where a tractor was chugging through a field. "Where are we?"

"A sign back a ways said we just entered Iowa. Anyhow, Beavis was a little slow on the takeoff, if you know what I mean, so he didn't know that Annabell had her reasons, and they were none too honorable, for looking for Elvis. That woman had bedroom eyes, and she clamped them on Billy the second she saw him."

Kane shook his head to clear it. They were in Iowa? That meant he'd been asleep for at least three hours. He wondered if Josie had been talking the entire time. He felt a little fuzzy. Exhaustion, injury and Josie's incessant talking could do that to a man. Hell, Josie's incessant talking could do that all by itself.

"'Course, Annabell isn't the only woman to set her sights on Billy. James, Roy and J.D., either, for that matter. Something about my brothers instills romance in the hearts of women, but females seem to like Billy the best."

She downshifted, then cast him a smile that was so full of pride and softness it made him feel dizzy *and* fuzzy at the same time.

"Billy doesn't seem to notice. Personally I think that's what the women in Hawk Hallow find so appealing about him."

She didn't appear to expect any comment from Kane. It was just as well. He would have had a hard time piecing together an intelligent answer. It was Josie. Lord, the woman never shut up. In fact, there was only one thing he could think of that would make her stop talking. His gaze strayed to the front of her shirt. Scowling, he shifted in his seat.

She'd been wearing the pink dress when they'd left Hawk Hallow. He couldn't recall seeing her change into her faded jeans and the soft purple shirt that rustled with her slightest movement. In his mind he could see her the way she'd been in the mountain cabin the day before. Standing in the bath, naked and wet and willing. Oh, yes, she'd been willing. A few more seconds without interruption and they would have…she would have…he would have…

"Billy always was a one-woman man. The poor guy has been pining after Lydia for more than two years now."

It took a while for her words to register through the haziness in Kane's brain. Billy. A one-woman man. And the little boy who looked nothing like the other McCoys. "Did this Lydia have red hair?" he asked.

She glanced at him and cast him a sad sort of smile that made him suck in a ragged breath. "As red as Tyler's."

"Tyler? That's the boy's name? I figured it would be Bubba or Junior or Red." Before she could get huffy, he said, "No offense intended."

Her hundred-watt smile hit him between the eyes. "No offense taken," she said quietly. "It was Billy who gave Tyler his name. Tyler was Lydia's last name, you see."

Was? "What happened to her?"

The truck started to shake, reminding Josie that she had to keep her foot on the gas pedal unless she wanted to shift into a lower gear. It wasn't easy to concentrate on driving when Kane was looking at her as if he wanted to do more than look, when his voice dipped so low she could feel it sweeping across her senses, when he forgot to put up the barriers and she could glimpse the part of him she'd fallen in love with.

"Josie?"

"Hmm?" She studied him thoughtfully for a moment, thinking there was something lazy and seductive in the way he was watching her, thinking she liked it very, very much.

"What happened to her?"

"What happened to who?"

A semi's horn blared. Josie swerved. And Kane swore.

"Watch where you're going, for God's sake. Are you trying to get us killed?"

She pulled over to the side of the highway. Shaking, she turned her head and slowly shook it. "You distracted me."

He raked his fingers through his hair then jerked his door open. "That does it. I'm driving."

She scooted over and let him have the wheel. But his gruffness didn't fool her. He wanted her. He had yesterday up in the mountain cabin, and he had a few minutes ago. Tucking the knowledge in the back of her mind for now, she continued her former story as if she hadn't taken a breather after nearly sideswiping an eighteen-wheeler.

"Lydia left the mountain right after Tyler was born. Billy doesn't know if she's alive or dead. He says if she's alive, she'll come back. Daddy and the boys don't think so. And I just don't know. It's been over two years already. Where could she be?"

She wasn't expecting a reply, and she didn't get one. As long as Kane continued to respond to her in other ways, Josie didn't mind. They stopped and ate when they got hungry, used rest rooms when they needed to, stretched their legs from time to time and took turns driving.

Josie would have *liked* a shower, she would have *loved* to rent a room and she would have *killed* to have at least a one-night honeymoon and actually consummate her marriage. It seemed Kane had other ideas. Consequently Josie slept through most of Minnesota, and drove through most of North Dakota.

With Kane at the wheel once again, she stared out the window for a long time, lost in her own thoughts. Her new husband wasn't much of a conversationalist. That was okay. She figured he would learn.

They passed through miles and miles of ranching country where huge herds of cattle roamed the gently rolling plains. Smiling at the way the calves frolicked in the early-morning sunshine, Josie said, "So this is big sky country."

She supposed she would have to be sitting still to appreciate the full effect. Chewing on her lower lip, she was silent and thoughtful, wondering about the place Kane lived. "How big is your ranch?"

"Just under four thousand acres, but it's more Spence's ranch than mine. And Gwen's. And the kids'."

Josie mulled his answer over for a while, contemplating the deep timbre of Kane's voice. He hadn't sounded bitter or angry or resentful when he'd mentioned his brother. So why wouldn't the Triple S be as much his as anybody's?

She'd known he had two brothers, one two years older, the other five years younger, but until that moment Josie hadn't thought about the possibility that he might have an extended family back in Montana. Staring out the window where purple wildflowers were waving in the spring breeze, she decided this called for some serious interrogations. "Is Gwen your sister-in-law?" she asked for starters.

Taking his grunt to mean "yes," she said, "How many kids do Spence and Gwen have?"

As usual, his answer was slow in coming. "Two. Both girls. Another baby on the way."

She turned her head slowly so she could watch his expression. "What about your other brother?"

"What about him?"

She congratulated herself on keeping her eyes from rolling back in her head. "Is Trace married?"

"Nope. No wife. And no kids that I know of."

"What about you?"

"What about me?"

"How many kids do you want?"

Kane didn't want to, but he couldn't seem to keep from glancing at Josie. "Kids?"

The woman-soft smile she gave him sliced through him a few inches left of the wound in his shoulder.

"Yes, you know," she said, smiling again. "Children. Little boys and girls with blond hair like me and brown eyes like you."

"I'm not having kids, Josie."

"How can you be so sure? I mean, you're physically able. You said so yourself."

"Trust me on this one. I know what I'm talking about."

"But—"

The firm shake of his head silenced her. "This isn't a fairy tale. After what you told me about your brother, you should know that better than anybody."

"After what I told you about *which* brother?" she asked.

"Billy. You see, it doesn't matter whether that woman— Lydia—is alive or not. If she wanted to come back, she would have, and your brother had better face it."

"Then you think Billy should forget about her and get on with his life?"

"It doesn't matter what I think. What is, is."

"Come on, Kane. Have a heart."

They were driving over Slater land now, the familiar surroundings seeping into Kane's senses the way a spring rain seeped into plowed ground. He didn't want to hurt Josie, but *he* wasn't the one who'd coerced *her* into marriage. Looking into eyes that had darkened to the color of smoke, he said, "Haven't you figured it out yet?"

"Haven't I figured what out yet?"

He forced his eyes back to the road just as the gate leading to the Triple S came into view. Bouncing through a rut in the driveway, he said, "I don't have a heart. You would be wise to keep that in mind."

His words held warning. That much was clear. Josie wanted to ask him what he was warning her against, but her gaze caught on the whiteness of his skin and the dark circles under his eyes, and she held her tongue.

Children's voices carried to her ears through Kane's open window. He threw the shifting lever out of gear, set the parking brake, cut the engine and opened his door. He had reached the front of the truck when Josie noticed two little girls prancing down the porch steps of a big white house. A woman, obviously pregnant, and a man who bore a striking resemblance to Kane were close on their heels.

Josie opened her own door and joined Kane in the middle of the gravel driveway. There was an awkward stretch of silence during which everybody seemed to be looking at Kane.

"What's wrong?" the woman asked him. "You're as white as a ghost."

Kane's deep sigh spoke volumes. "I'm fine, Gwen. Everybody," he finally declared, "this is Josie Slater. My wife."

Josie saw the shock on the pretty woman's face. The same expression was mirrored on the husband's. She glanced at Kane, wishing he would say something to break the tension. Finally he did. "Josie took me in after I was shot during a bounty hunt gone wrong. I'm going to live, but right now I'm dead tired. I'm going to bed."

Cradling his right arm in his left hand, he turned. Without so much as another word or a backward glance, he ambled away toward a weathered building that looked as if it could have been used as a bunkhouse in years gone by.

For several seconds the only sound to break the quiet was the slamming of that bunkhouse's screen door. Eyeing the strangers who were her new family, Josie tried to smile.

"As far as explanations go, that one could have used a little work. Kane's a man of few words, isn't he?"

Two little girls who looked to be about four and five stared up at Josie as if they weren't accustomed to seeing strangers out here in the middle of nowhere. The man and woman exchanged a meaningful look. One hand on her protruding stomach, the other at the small of her back, the woman was the first to find her voice. "Hi. I'm Gwen Slater. That man putting his eyes back in their sockets is my husband, Spence. These two are our girls, Mallory and Melissa. Girls, say hello to your new Aunt Josie."

The girls said hello then hid behind their mother. Kane's older brother offered Josie his hand. His handshake was firm, his gaze steady. Gwen elbowed her way in front of him, her blue eyes crinkling with laughter and her short dark hair blowing across her cheek. "I don't know how you did it, but welcome to the Triple S. Why don't you come inside? There's coffee left, and enough pancake batter to fix you a nice, tall stack."

Josie liked the warmth and sincerity in Gwen's eyes and the slight unevenness of her teeth when she smiled. Glancing at the weathered, gray building in the distance, she said, "Thanks, but I think I'd better check on Kane."

She started toward the bunkhouse, only to turn suddenly and say, "If it's okay I'd like to stop by a little later. You have no idea what a relief it is to see a friendly face."

Gwen shook her head. "Hold on to your relief, and if I were you, I'd conserve your strength. Now that you're married to a Slater, you're going to need it more than you can imagine."

The stern look Spence gave his wife was a dead ringer for the kind of look Kane had already given Josie a dozen times. Gwen appeared as unfazed by it as Josie was. The short, dark haired woman looped her arm through her husband's and drew him with her toward the house, the little girls prancing on ahead of them. Josie continued on toward the bunkhouse. The landscape in the distance was unfamiliar, but womanhood and sisterhood were universal. She already had one friend in Montana. No matter what Gwen said about holding on to her relief, Josie's step was lighter by the time she'd reached the screen door.

Kane opened his eyes. For a moment he thought he was in the mountain cabin. But there was no snow outside the window and this was his bed. Ah, yes. He was back at the Triple S.

He swung his feet to the floor and sat up. His shoulder felt better, and he was starving. His gaze fell upon a stack of newspapers. *Sunday.* Could he really have been asleep for three days? He remembered falling across the bed and closing his eyes. Everything after that was a little fuzzy. Vaguely he recalled sipping something cool every now and then, and he was pretty sure Doc Jenkins had checked him over.

He was halfway to the bathroom before it dawned on him that he was naked. Nothing unusual about sleeping in the raw. Except this time he'd gone to bed fully clothed. Josie must have undressed him.

Josie.

His stomach growled at the same time he did. It was a damn symphony. He couldn't help it. The thought of Josie had that effect on him. It had another effect on him, too.

Still, he thought, donning a pair of jeans and plodding out to the kitchen. It was still good to be home.

He'd moved out here to the old bunkhouse right after Spence and Gwen got married ten years ago. Before setting off for places unknown, Trace had lived here, too. He still bunked down here whenever he was passing through.

Spence and Gwen had both insisted it wasn't necessary, that the big house would always be their home, too. Kane appreciated the sentiment, but he preferred it out here. He answered to no one, coming and going as he pleased. He liked to keep his life simple, and the bunkhouse suited his needs. There was a phone, an answering machine, a little furniture, a few dishes and not much else. He didn't care if the place was old and a little on the rustic side. Early squalor. That's how a woman he'd dated a few years back had described it.

He sniffed... What the hell? Since when had the air smelled of lemons? And what in blazes were curtains doing at the windows?

It didn't take a mastermind to figure out who was responsible. Josie's signature was on everything, from the chili bubbling on the ancient electric stove to the homemade bread cooling on a towel to the jelly jar of wildflowers on the windowsill. Leave it to a woman to try to turn a perfectly fine bunkhouse into a home. The place had *wife* written all over it. His mind went blank as if short-circuited. Dazedly he sliced off a thick wedge of bread and headed for the bathroom. Josie may have had some annoying tendencies, but she sure could cook.

A warning voice sounded in his ears, reminding him not to get too used to the situation. Because that was all this was. A situation, a brief period of time stuck between what had happened last week and what would happen next week or next month or next year.

He stared at his reflection in the mirror. Deciding it was time to do something about the bleary-eyed person staring back at him, he got busy. Ten minutes later the whiskers were gone. Thanks to his trusty electric razor, his face was nick-free. Several days' worth of grime had been washed down the shower drain. Feeling more human, he reached for a clean pair of jeans. Kane did a double take. Not only were his jeans and shirts clean, but they were folded and stacked in neat piles. Even his sock drawer was organized. Obviously Josie had been very busy. She probably thought she'd been doing him a favor.

Kane knew then and there that he had to make her understand that this arrangement was far from permanent. He had to end things before she got too attached. He wasn't worried about himself. Once upon a time he'd gotten attached to people and places. Not anymore. These days, Kane Slater was immune.

Kane let the screen door bang shut behind him. Shading his eyes with one hand, he could see Spence in the distance, his lasso raised, his horse galloping, cattle bawling. Kane almost smiled, because every now and then he could hear one or two succinct cuss words all the way from here. Gwen would give Spence a good tongue-lashing if she heard. Not that Spence would stop. After all, Kane's older brother was every bit as stubborn as he was. As far as Kane was concerned, a little stubbornness was a good thing. Gwen didn't agree. Hell, Josie probably wouldn't, either. Where was that woman, anyway?

He glanced all around him. Deciding she was probably in the big house with Gwen and the girls, he ambled in that direction until an unfamiliar sound slowed his steps. Eyes narrowed, he tried to place the rhythmic *swish*-swish-*swish*-swish tune carrying to his ears on the breeze. He followed the sound around the bunkhouse, straight to the weathered barn.

His boots scudded on the rotting floorboards inside the old tack room, and dust particles floated on a ray of sunshine slanting through a hole in the roof. Josie was bent over a sawhorse, one hand holding a piece of wood firmly in place, the other gliding a piece of sandpaper over it. Her hair hung in front of her shoulder, hiding her expression from his view, the long tresses swinging back and forth every time she made another pass with the sandpaper. She was wearing what looked like one of his white shirts. The sleeves were rolled up, the tails tied at her waist. Her jeans were faded and worn, delineating the muscles in her thighs and the curve of her backside.

His hands moved at his side, as if spreading wide exactly where he was looking. That did it. He *had* to put a stop to this craziness here and now. He would tell her, in no uncertain terms, that he wasn't the marrying kind. If all went well, she would be on a train or a bus before nightfall.

He took a step toward her, thinking, yes, that's what he would do—thank her for saving his life and explain that she would be better off without him.

Her hair swished, and her backside wiggled slightly.

Kane swallowed.

He would be firm but gentle. She was young, after all. And innocent. He gulped.

He had to tell her, and he had to do it now. Just jump right in with no *ands, ifs, or buts*. Just the facts. Sorry and so long.

He opened his mouth to speak, but she must have seen him out of the corner of her eye because she spun around to face him. That ray of sunlight caught on her hair, and he couldn't remember what he was going to say.

As usual, Josie had no such trouble. "Well, looky who's awake. I told Gwen I was beginning to think you were going to sleep until fall, like a bear in reverse. Hello. Feeling better?"

He nodded, and he could only assume that whatever was cracking his face was his own smile. What was he doing out here? Oh, now he remembered. He was—*is*—going to tell her not to get too comfortable around here. He opened his mouth a second time, and heard himself say, "Where did you get the curtains?"

For crying out loud, where had that come from?

Grinning softly, she strode closer. "Gwen found them in a trunk in the attic. She said they used to be your mother's, and that your mama died when you were small."

Kane felt his eyes narrow a little more with every step Josie took. "I was eight. My father died when I was twenty-one. Growing old doesn't run in my family. That's why this will never work, Josie. We have to get a divorce, or an annulment, or whatever the hell it takes to end this here and now."

Josie thought there was a lot of meaning behind what he'd said. Not about getting a divorce or an annulment, but about the fact that growing old doesn't run in his family. Deciding it might be best to pursue the subject at a later date, she went back to the sawhorse and took up where she'd left off. "Aren't you going to ask me what I'm doing?" she asked.

"I know what you're doing, dammit. You're evading the issue."

"I'm building birdhouses." She pointed to the five houses, each of them different, she'd already finished. "Practically every yard in Hawk Hollow has one of my birdhouses or feeders. If you wouldn't have married me when you did, I would have been known as the *bird lady* forever and ever. You saved my life just as surely as I saved yours. Fate brought us together. Don't you see? This was all meant to be."

"This was *not* meant to be, dammit. And this sure as hell isn't permanent. I know I owe you for saving my life. I just don't know how to repay that kind of debt."

"You want to repay me?"

She heard his boots thudding to the other side of the room. Moments later, he said, "You can have half my bank balance."

Josie bristled. She was all set to give him a piece of her mind when curiosity took over. "How much money do you have in the bank?"

Kane smiled to himself. This was more like it. Now they were getting someplace. Shrugging his good shoulder, he said, "Fifty thousand. There would have been more if my latest felon hadn't gotten away. Still, fifty thousand isn't bad. Half of that would be enough to get you started seeing the world."

She stared at him for so long he felt uneasy. Finally she said, "I don't want your money, Kane."

"Well, you can't have half of the ranch. Trace and I deeded our shares to Spence a long time ago. No attorney in the world could get it back for you and even if one could, I'd fight you every step of the—"

"I don't want your ranch, either."

He stopped short. "You don't?"

She shook her head.

"Then what do you want?"

Josie stared at Kane, wondering how much she should say. She thought about telling him she didn't want anything, but she'd never been very good at lying, and she really didn't see any point in trying to perfect it now. Sashaying closer, she laid her hand on his sore arm. Keeping her touch featherlight and her voice as soft as a caress, she whispered, "Why, Kane, I already told you. I want you."

Chapter Six

"You want me." Kane's voice was deep, and huskier than he would have liked. Josie was looking up at him as if enthralled by what she saw. It was disconcerting. Hell, it was arousing.

"Is that so hard to fathom?" she whispered. "A woman wanting you?"

He swore under his breath. Hell no, being wanted by a woman wasn't hard to fathom. Other women had wanted him over the years. There was that woman from Topeka—what was her name? And that aspiring model from California—Krissy, or Mindy, or Sissy, or something.

Kane felt a headache coming on. This should have been simple, but he was beginning to realize that nothing was simple with Josie. It wasn't that she wasn't bright. She was amazingly well-read and well-informed for a girl from the hills who had little in the way of higher education. No, the problem wasn't with her. He was the one with the problem, because it seemed that he couldn't think straight whenever he came within fifteen feet of her.

Willing the grogginess in his head to clear, he took a backward step and strode to a makeshift shelf where he examined the birdhouses Josie had built. Three of them had roofs made out of bark and were fashioned into rustic-style houses. One looked like a church, complete with a steeple and one was reminiscent of an old-fashioned general store. The workmanship was amazing, Josie's eye for detail evident in every piece. He wondered where she'd acquired her skill, and fleetingly tried to recall if he'd ever dated another woman who liked to build things. Damn, he couldn't remember that, either.

Okay, maybe he couldn't remember the names of the women he'd seen over the years or some of the more pertinent details of their personalities, but he remembered the lengthy conversations he'd had with them following their declarations of love. After he'd explained that he wasn't the forever type, a woman usually cried. He hated tears, but he would have hated to lead someone on even more. A woman tended to grow tired of having a relationship with a man who could offer her no future. More often than not, she stopped calling or stopping by. Sooner or later he usually heard that she'd married somebody else.

"*Is* being wanted so hard to fathom, Kane?"

The sound of Josie's voice behind him brought him out of his reverie. Scowling, he said, "I haven't been living the life of a monk, if that's what you're asking."

There. Let her chew on that for a while. Maybe if he made her angry she would face the facts and agree that this had been a mistake.

"It's nice to know that at least one of us has had some fun. What we were doing in the mountain cabin *was* fun, wasn't it?"

Fun? Was that what she called it? He made the mistake of giving her a sidelong glance, and found her looking up at him, a come-hither light in her eyes, a tender smile on her lips. He would only have to bend slightly and lower his face to hers, to cover her lips with his. One smooth movement, and the rest would be history, their marriage would be consummated and he would find relief, at least for a little while. Just one dip, one kiss that could change the course of the rest of his life.

Josie was so engrossed in the changes taking place in Kane's expression that she was only marginally aware that he was looking at her, too. My, he was a striking man; his lips were parted slightly, his jaw square, his nose straight. His skin had lost its pallor and his eyes held a sheen that made her wonder if he might be imagining the way things had been in that mountain cabin, too, when he'd kissed her and touched her and had lain naked with her, when she'd wrapped her hands around him, and when they'd been but a moment away from making love.

She wanted to recapture that moment, and sensed that he wanted that, too. Just thinking about it made her eager. Raising up on tiptoe, she whispered, "I fashioned one of my birdhouses after the mountain cabin. I'd like you to have it, as a wedding present from me. Is there anything you'd like to give to me?"

Kane recognized the swooping pull low in his body, and he knew what he wanted to do about it. He had no idea where such a small woman got so much nerve, but if he wasn't careful, he was going to lose the last shred of his control. He raised his hand in a halting gesture. Josie took it in one of hers and gently cradled it against her cheek. Slowly she turned her head, pressing a kiss into his palm.

Kane heard a ringing in his ears and felt a chugging in his chest. "Josie, I don't think—"

"Shh," she whispered, feathering kisses on his wrist, on the sensitive skin on the inside of his forearm, on up to his chin, his cheek, the edge of his mouth. "Gwen told me you Slaters think too much. Don't think, Kane. Touch, and be touched, feel, and be felt, give to me, and take from me."

Her soft voice worked over his senses, her hands working over his flesh. Maybe she was right. Maybe he did think too much. That much thinking could leave a man with an enormous need. It didn't require much conscious thought to know what to do about a need like that. Of their own volition, his fingers went to the buttons on her shirt, deftly unfastening them.

Her head tipped back when he slid his hand inside her shirt. He cupped her bare breast. And she sighed.

"Ah, Kane, Gwen gives very good advice."

The feel of her breast in his hand sent a chain reaction across his body. "I'd be wary of taking advice from Gwen if I were you," he rasped, moving on to her other breast.

Eyes closed, Josie swayed slightly. "She's been wonderful," she whispered, "taking me under her wing, and all. But she's very protective of you. Spence is, too, for that matter. It makes me wonder what secret they're guarding."

"Secret?"

"Hmm. When you first stumbled into the mountain cabin I thought you might have been an ax murderer. Since I doubt they'd let murderers be bounty hunters, I've decided it must be something else. Maybe you were abducted by aliens or something."

He spread her shirt wide. After taking an admiring look, he closed his eyes. Drawing her tight to his body, he almost smiled. "Hardly," he whispered huskily. "What you see is exactly what you get."

"What I see," she whispered on a sigh, her fingers unfastening his top button, "is a rugged man with a deep hunger and a deeper need."

Kane felt himself going very still. Need? Him?

He took a backward step. Pulling her hands from around his neck, he slowly brought them between their bodies. He'd almost given in to the invitation in her eyes. He'd almost ignored his better judgment and his instincts.

"Kane, what is it? What's wrong?"

He released her wrists and turned on his heel, all in one motion. When he glanced over his shoulder, her shirt was still open. Scowling, he strode to the makeshift shelf. Keeping his back to her, he said, "I have to go to Butte."

"Where?"

"Butte."

"I heard you. I meant when?"

"Now."

"Now, as in right this minute?"

She must have noticed his slight nod, because she said, "Why?"

Getting his breathing under control, he said, "I have to file a report with the head of the Bail Enforcement Agency."

"But, Kane, you're still weak, and your shoulder hasn't healed."

"My shoulder's fine. I'm fine. I can take care of myself, Josie. I've been doing it for a long time."

He made it to the door in three long strides.

"How long will you be gone?" she called to his back.

He waited to turn around until after he'd stepped outside. Even then, he wished he'd put more distance between them. Josie was standing in that ray of sunshine now, the dust particles suspended in thin air, as unmoving as she was. Sunlight spilled over her blond hair, glinting off her white shirt, casting a warm glow across her pale cheeks. Her eyes held a strange mixture of hurt and longing. A dangerous combination in any woman. A powerful, deadly one in Josie.

No, he thought vehemently. The only power a woman had over him was the power he gave her. Girded with renewed resolve, he said, "I don't know how long this will take. Don't wait up."

Without another word, he was gone, and Josie was left standing in a patch of sunshine, her nose itching, her eyes smarting. She crossed her arms, sniffled and promptly buttoned her shirt.

What in Sam Hill just happened?

One minute Kane had been kissing her and touching her and wanting her, and the next thing she knew he'd been fighting it with everything he had. She sniffled again, but she didn't give in to tears. Turning in a circle, she studied her surroundings very carefully. Everything looked the same as it had five minutes ago. Her birdhouses sat on a sagging shelf, old bridles and reins and horseshoes hanging on nails on the wall.

What had she done to cause Kane to pull away? What had she said? She combed her mind, thinking.

He'd reacted favorably to her mention of the mountain cabin. What an understatement. He'd practically had her out of her shirt in five seconds flat. What little experience she had with passion had come from Kane, himself. And he'd wanted her. She'd seen it in his eyes, felt it in his touch, not to mention where he'd pressed her tight to his body.

It wasn't long before she heard an engine rumble to life. She didn't have to walk to the door to know Kane was driving away. She wondered how far it was to Butte. And she wondered if it had really been necessary for Kane to go there.

Just who was this man she'd married?

Until a few days ago, she'd thought she understood men. She'd certainly believed she knew what made them behave the way they did. Compared to Kane, her brothers had been very predictable. There had been a lot of noise in the McCoy household while she'd been growing up, but very few surprises. Even as adults, the McCoy boys were relatively easy to get along with. *Sex and supper,* her brother, Roy, had always said, *could make a man happy for life.*

Josie dropped her sandpaper and hurried from the barn and into the bunkhouse. When her eyes had adjusted to the dim interior, she saw that the chili she'd prepared earlier was still bubbling on the stove, untouched, which meant that Kane hadn't eaten before he'd gone. He hadn't given in to his other need, either. So much for Roy's credibility.

Understanding Kane was going to require insight and knowledge. If she would have been back on her mountain, she would have gone to Minerva Jones or Nellie Peters or Edwina Gilson for advice. Suddenly, Josie knew what she had to do. Brushing the sanding dust from her hands, she turned the burner off and pushed through the door. Following the sound of children's voices raised in play, Josie strode to the big white house and the only other grown woman for miles and miles.

"When Orin's wife found out, she clobbered him over the head with a frying pan. Put a goose egg the size of a walnut smack-dab in the middle of his forehead. Nellie Peters said she should have hit him someplace else, but Polly sniffed and said a woman has to have some scruples. I suppose she's…"

Josie's voice trailed away. Glancing across the room, she caught Gwen looking at her strangely. "I'm boring you to death, aren't I?"

"Are you kidding?" Gwen exclaimed, patting her round

abdomen with one hand and pointing to her sleeping daughters with the other. "If it wasn't so much work to get out of this chair, I'd kiss you. All your talking has put Mallory and Melissa to sleep."

Josie glanced around the small room. She'd been talking to Gwen for the better part of an hour. The girls *had* fallen asleep on opposite ends of the sofa. Even the family dog, a big yellow mutt named Bowser was snoring in a patch of sunshine.

"You have a nice voice," Gwen said quietly. "But you'd better ask what it is you came over to ask before they wake up again."

Josie glanced up from the lukewarm coffee in front of her, straight into Gwen Slater's warm blue eyes. Shrugging a little sheepishly, Josie said, "I've been accused of talking a mile a minute all my life. When it comes to Kane, I don't know where to begin."

"That's understandable," Gwen answered after a time. "The two of you got off to a rocky start."

Josie released a breath of pent-up air. "You have no idea how rocky."

"Most people out here like their privacy. That's why I haven't pried. But if you *wanted* to tell me, I'd be happy to listen." Gwen shifted on the cushioned chair, searching for a more comfortable position.

After studying her thumbnail for an inordinate amount of time, Josie said, "I could use a little insight into the Slater men in general. Kane in particular."

Gwen was quiet for a long time. Finally she said, "How well do you know Kane, Josie?"

"Well enough to love him. Not well enough to understand him. He stumbled into my mountain cabin during a blizzard thirteen days ago. His right side was covered with blood and he was delirious and half-frozen. I put him to bed and nursed him back to health. We were married by the justice of the peace a few days ago. In lieu of a honeymoon, we drove straight through all the way from Hawk Hollow, Tennessee.''

Gwen whistled softly. ''Why do I have the feeling you're leaving a lot out? The justice of the peace married you? I'm trying to picture that.''

''It wasn't a conventional wedding ceremony, but my daddy gave me away, and my brothers were there. You could say they served as my bridesmaids, only instead of bouquets, they each carried a shotgun.''

Gwen's eyes grew large, only to crinkle as her surprise gave way to laughter. ''Oh, Josie, that's priceless. Imagine the stories you'll be able to tell your grandchildren someday.''

Josie's harrumph was so loud it stirred the dog into opening one bloodshot eye. While Bowser settled back into his nap, Josie said, ''A person has to have *children* before she can have *grandchildren*. At the rate I'm going, I'll still be a virgin when I'm sixty-five.''

Gwen was looking at Josie the way a lot of people looked at Josie, eyebrows raised, mouth open, thoughts careening in a desperate attempt to understand what she was talking about. ''Are you telling me your father forced Kane to marry you even though the two of you didn't—''

Josie nodded. After a time, a sheepish grin slid across her face. ''We almost did. Boy, you wouldn't believe how close we came. I've tried since then, and he's wanted to, but every time I think we're getting close, he up and leaves.''

''That,'' Gwen said, ''is the Slater way.''

''Then Kane's behavior is normal?''

''It's normal for a Slater. How much do you know about Kane's past?''

Skewing her mouth to one side, Josie thought very carefully about the few tidbits of information Kane had shared with her concerning his past. "He hasn't said much, but he seems to have a great respect for Spence and a great fondness for Trace. You're the one who told me their mother died when they were all boys. I know how it feels to lose a mother."

Gwen's gaze rested on each of her daughters. Nodding, she whispered, "I grew up in Butternut, and I remember how folks talked after Selma Slater died. Suddenly Harve had three boys to raise and a ranch to run. He did his best, and when he died, the boys reacted the way their father had before them, by withdrawing into themselves. Trace left home when he was barely eighteen. He calls now and then, and shows up when we least expect him. As the oldest, Spence took on the responsibility of the ranch. In the early days of our marriage, he used to ride off into the sunset without warning. I never knew how long he would be gone."

"And Kane took up bounty hunting," Josie said, beginning to understand.

"They're a quiet, brooding lot, that's for sure," Gwen said. "It takes a bighearted woman to love them. But they're worth it, Josie."

"I *know that*," Josie stated emphatically. "I just don't know how I'm going to get him to love me back."

"I don't know about Kane," Gwen said in a conspiratorial whisper, "but over the years I've found that Spence is the most acquiescent when I keep him a little off balance."

Josie leaned forward. "What do you mean by off balance?"

Gwen wiggled her eyebrows a few times and winked.

"For instance, Spence thinks having this baby was his idea."

"And it wasn't?"

"Heavens no, but I'm not going to be the one to tell him different."

Josie studied Gwen's features unhurriedly. The dimples in the other woman's face made her appear younger than her thirty-two years. Her hair was nearly black and chin length, her smile was artful, serene. If a person looked hard enough, she could see that it was also the tiniest bit beguiling. Leaning back in her chair, Josie said, "You're a very sneaky woman, do you know that?"

Struggling to stand, Gwen nodded knowingly. "Don't be disappointed if it takes a while with Kane. Just keep doing the last thing he expects. Then stand back and reap the rewards."

As Josie's mind raced ahead to the *rewards* she hoped to reap, she and Gwen walked outside. Gwen shaded her eyes with one hand, looking out over the horizon. Josie followed the course of her new sister-in-law's gaze until she saw Spence and his horse, galloping toward home a quarter mile away. Josie sighed, because Gwen Slater wasn't only smart and pretty. She was also very lucky. Josie wanted to be lucky like that. She wanted to be able to pick out her husband's lone form on the horizon, and feel warmed by the knowledge that he was coming home to her. She wanted to meet his gaze at the end of the day, sensing his mood, anticipating his embrace, welcoming him home. She wanted so many things, and Kane was at the center of them all.

Keep him off balance, Gwen had said. Hmm. How did a woman keep a bounty hunter who was as surefooted as a mountain goat and just as stubborn off balance? Striding back to the bunkhouse, Josie was determined to find a way.

* * *

Josie wasn't sure what woke her, the crick in her neck or the ache in her back, but she opened her eyes and looked around. Pushing herself to a sitting position, she lowered her feet to the floor. She didn't remember falling asleep, but she remembered brushing her hair and dabbing perfume behind her ears and curling up on the sofa to wait for Kane to come home.

Kane.

Rats. It was morning. Where was he?

She was on her feet and down the hall, her mind conjuring up morbid details of car accidents and gunshots and bar fights. She stopped in the doorway of Kane's room and felt herself relax. Kane's holster and gun hung on a peg near the door. His blankets had been pulled up haphazardly, but it was obvious that his bed had been slept in. Although she hadn't heard him come in, at least he'd been home.

Wondering where he was now, she hurried into the bathroom. It only took a few swipes with the brush to restore a little order to her hair, but it was going to take time to remove the imprint the sofa cushion had left on her cheek.

Now what? she thought, meandering back the way she'd come. She crossed her arms then casually glanced out the window where the pale gray of early dawn was creeping across the sky. A light in the barn caught her attention. Acting on impulse, she hurried out the door. By the time she reached the barn, her bare feet were cold and wet from the heavy dew. Shivering, she slipped inside.

The air was slightly warmer in the barn, the smell of hay and oats as comforting as the nickers and neighs of the horses, and the low, smooth baritone bidding them good morning. Josie found herself smiling, her heart brimming with emotion at the tenderness in Kane's voice, and in the way his hand stroked the animals as he passed. His touch was so gentle. How could he not see that he deserved a gentle touch in return?

He kept his back to her as he heaved a saddle from its rack and awkwardly swung it onto a big black horse he called Stalker. When the bridle was in place and the saddle was cinched tight, Josie strolled closer. The horse noticed her first, but she was more interested in the heat in Kane's gaze. It reminded her that she was wearing a pale blue nightgown that clung to her slight curves, leaving little room for imagination. She didn't have to glance down to know what the cold had done to her body. Kane's reaction said it all.

"Good morning," she called, stopping a few feet away. "What time did you get in?"

He turned his attention back to his horse, but she'd seen the way his throat had convulsed on a swallow. "Around three. Didn't see any reason to wake you."

"I can think of one reason, Kane."

His hand stilled for only an instant, but it was enough to let her know that he was aware of her meaning. "You couldn't have gotten much sleep," she said. "Do you really have to go out on the range right now? Wouldn't you rather come back to bed?"

Kane's heart pounded and his pulse quickened. He knew he'd made an error in judgment the instant he turned to face Josie. She was looking up at him, her eyes full of warmth and so much obvious invitation even a moron could see. Her lips quivered slightly on a shiver, and goose bumps danced across her shoulders. God help him, he was tempted to wrap his arms around her and warm her every way he knew.

He hadn't been sure what to expect when he'd arrived home three hours ago, but it hadn't been the sight of Josie fast asleep on the threadbare couch, her hair falling across her pillow, her face pale in repose, looking soft and sexy as hell. She would never know how long he'd stood there, fighting with his conscience. Scowling, he realized he was fighting with it again.

Oh, for crying out loud. He stomped around Stalker and swung into the saddle. Peering down at Josie, he said, "This ranch doesn't run on its own, you know."

Hurt flickered across her face as she said, "I didn't mean to imply that it did. I'm just a little out of sorts, that's all. I don't know how you get by on so little sleep."

There was only one thing Kane could think of that was worse than unspent desire, and that was guilt. Releasing a deep breath, he lowered his voice and said, "I have to go, Josie. Spence rode out fifteen minutes ago. He's expecting me to help."

He felt her eyes on him as he turned Stalker and headed for the door. Glancing over his shoulder, he said, "By the way, you don't have to sleep on the sofa anymore."

"I don't?"

He pulled at the brim of his brown Stetson. "You can sleep in my bed—"

Josie felt as if the fog in her head was clearing. She didn't care how idiotic she looked. She felt her smile broaden.

"Until the divorce papers arrive, I'll sleep in the spare room. Trace is the only one who uses it, and he hasn't been home in a dog's age."

"You've already seen someone about a divorce?" she asked shakily.

"It's faster than an annulment. It's for the best, Josie. Believe me."

He ducked when he went through the door, the sound of hoofbeats echoing in Josie's ears as she watched him ride out of sight.

Josie felt disappointed. Worse, she felt bereft. A divorce was for the best, he'd said. The best for who? Not for her. Surely not for him. How could he divorce her when he hadn't even given himself a chance to love her? Everyone needed love, didn't they? Even stubborn bounty hunters with wounded shoulders and barricaded hearts.

The clattering of her teeth brought her from her musings. This wasn't over, she thought, making a mad dash for the warmth of the bunkhouse. She'd planned to keep Kane so off balance that he would tumble straight into her arms. It looked as if she was going to have to hurry if she was going to accomplish it before divorce papers arrived.

Her mind raced ahead. The poor man wouldn't know what hit him. The poor, stubborn, thickheaded, contrary, maddening man.

Kane leaned into the thick board, Spence's hammer sinking a long nail in three blows. "What did Karl Kennedy have to say about the report you filed?"

Kane shrugged one shoulder and heaved another board into place. "He chewed me out for not wearing a bullet-proof vest and told me to keep my butt home until my shoulder's completely healed. When he finished with his lecture, he escorted me to the hospital for X rays."

"And?" Spence prodded.

"And my shoulder's going to be fine. A physical therapist gave me a ball to squeeze to help me get the strength back in my grip. I told her I didn't need any physical therapy."

"That figures," Spence said, eyeing the work they'd accomplished. "Let's call it a day."

Kane released a deep breath and hoisted himself to the top of the fence he and Spence had just mended. He'd put in a full day of work on the ranch, and he felt it in every muscle. He hated to admit it, but he was exhausted. This weakness was as frustrating as hell. He had strict orders to exercise his hand four times a day. Kane wasn't sure he had the energy to walk to the bunkhouse, let alone exercise his injured arm. Sitting down felt good. Sleep was going to feel even better.

The sound of laughter had him fumbling in his pocket for a pack of cigarettes. A moment later a match flickered, the smell of sulfur carrying to his nostrils seconds before nicotine found its way to his lungs.

"I thought you quit," Spence said, crossing his arms over the top of the fence a few feet away.

Kane shrugged and took another deep draw on his cigarette. He'd quit a dozen times, and would probably quit a dozen more.

"Gwen will have your hide," Spence declared.

Both their gazes strayed to the side yard where Josie and Gwen were trying to nail a birdhouse onto a post they'd set into the ground. Tipping his hat back with one finger, Spence shook his head. "That woman won't listen to a thing I say. Look at her out there, dancing around as if she was a newlywed and not eight months pregnant with our third child. She refuses to slow down. This pregnancy is different than the first two. She's bigger, and she tires more easily."

Kane hadn't realized he'd allowed his gaze to stray to Josie's blond hair until he had to force his eyes to his sister-in-law's rounded abdomen. "Maybe this one will be a boy."

He sensed more than saw his brother's shrug. "I think Gwen has a feeling about it. I'll just be glad when it's over. I must have been out of my mind to suggest having another one."

On the other side of the driveway, four females were

making enough racket for ten people as they secured the birdhouse to its post. The men looked on in silence, smoke curling above their heads. Spence was the first to speak. "She reminds me of somebody."

"Gwen?"

"No, Josie."

"Don't tell me she reminds you of Mom."

"Not Mom. Maggie."

Kane took a long draw on his cigarette. Unfortunately the nicotine did little to steady his erratic heartbeat. "Maggie had black hair."

"I know. It's not her looks. It's Josie's laughter. Maggie used to laugh like that. Remember?"

Kane went perfectly still. He hadn't thought about Maggie in a long time, but he hadn't forgotten. How could a man forget the first woman he'd ever loved?

As if sensing he'd said enough, Spence pushed away from the fence and slowly made his way toward his wife and daughters. Kane's heart was still chugging when he glanced up, straight into Josie's eyes. He took another long draw on his cigarette as she walked toward him, but he didn't look away.

They hadn't spoken since slightly after dawn when he'd informed her that divorce papers were on the way. He'd caught a few glimpses of her throughout the day, but this was the first time he'd gotten a good, long look at her since she'd changed out of the thin gown she'd been wearing that morning.

Now, she was wearing faded brown jeans, a blue chambray shirt and a quilted vest. Steadily walking toward him, shoulders back, head held high, she had the look of a woman begging for trouble. And Kane knew without a doubt that trouble was exactly what he was in for.

* * *

Josie couldn't see Kane's eyes beneath the brim of his brown Stetson, but she felt them on her. His body language was deceiving, arms crossed, knees bent, heels resting on a lower board. It was easy to imagine him hanging out in back alleys, looking relaxed, comfortable, unaffected—an illusion he'd undoubtedly perfected somewhere along the way.

Josie knew when she was being ignored, and she knew when she was being avoided. Kane had been doing both all day. He was obviously expecting her to retaliate following the little bombshell he'd dropped concerning a divorce. She had other ideas.

"Howdy." Hiding a smile at Kane's obvious surprise, she ambled over to the fence. Resting one shoulder against a board, she folded her arms and made a point to breathe in a deep breath of fresh April air. "So this is big sky country. What do you call that mountain range?"

When he didn't answer, she said, "If you don't tell me I'll be forced to guess."

With a shake of his head, he said, "The Bear Paw Mountains are visible to the west, the Little Rocky Mountains to the south. Although you can't see it, the Milk River flows north of the Slater spread."

Josie kept her eyes trained in the distance. "And what's to the east?"

"What are you doing, Josie?"

She finally looked up at him, meeting the intensity in his gaze. "I'm talking. I always talk. You know that. Daddy says it's a curse, but I prefer to think of it as a gift. It's an enormous tension reliever, not to mention an icebreaker. I've been thinking."

She could tell by the way his jaw clenched and his eyes narrowed that he was expecting the worst. Look out. Here it comes, was written all over his face. "You've been thinking," he said, a cold edge of irony in his voice.

She made a humming sound that meant yes and said, "About a lot of things, but mostly about us."

"About us." She heard his boot creak and could practically hear his thoughts careening.

"More specifically," she said, looking away, into the distance. "About our relationship and what you told me this morning about getting a divorce."

"Josie—"

"And I've decided not to stand in your way."

Kane almost fell off the fence. "You're not?"

She shook her head, albeit sadly. "This was all my fault in the first place—Daddy and the boys forcing you to marry me when you didn't…we didn't…I still haven't…"

Kane tried to relax, but his heart chugged to life. After that, the changes taking place elsewhere in his body made relaxing out of the question.

"Anyway," she was saying, "I want you to know I'm sorry. I only did it because I love you, and I wanted you to be my first lover."

He didn't know how long he'd been staring at Josie's mouth, but as he watched her lips move, he found himself wanting to kiss her, long and slow and deep, over and over and over.

She looked up at him, and wavered him a tremulous smile. "I still want you to be my first lover, but I'm not going to force anything on you that you don't want. Oh, and another thing—I think a person recovering from a gunshot wound should be allowed to sleep in his own bed. I'll just move my things to the spare room. If you change your mind, I want you to know you're welcome to join me anytime you want."

She reached up and touched his cheek with her fingertips,

skimming them over his lips, resting the pad of her middle finger along the shallow cleft in his chin. Kane didn't move, his eyes trained on her face. "Well, looky here," she whispered. "I seem to have run out of things to say. Will wonders never cease? I guess I'll go inside now. Night, Kane. Sweet dreams."

Kane might have answered, but it was more likely that he'd simply stared after her, mouth open, blood pounding through his veins. He didn't know how long he sat on the fence, his fingers curled into fists at his sides, his knees locked, his breathing ragged. Josie had claimed she'd run out of things to say, but he was the one who was speechless. He'd expected a tirade. It would have been easier to take than her sad smile.

Josie made it as far as the kitchen before her knees started to wobble. She clutched the back of a chair and tried to take a deep breath. That had *not* gone the way she'd planned. She'd rehearsed what she was going to say a dozen times and had opened her mouth to deliver her speech, and *whoosh,* out gushed all her emotions. Why, she'd planned to keep Kane off balance, not tell him she was sorry for tricking him into marrying her.

She supposed she'd still knocked him off balance. Unfortunately she felt topsy-turvy, too. And now it was too late to undo what she'd said. Divorce papers were due to arrive in a matter of weeks, and she'd given Kane her word that she wouldn't try to seduce him.

She stepped beneath the shower, sputtering that she needed her head examined. Her father was right. Her nonstop talking really was a curse. Drying off, she plodded to the spare bedroom. Eyeing the thin mattress and sparsely furnished room, she sank to the bed. The springs creaked beneath her weight, the blanket scratchy beneath her hand.

She rose to her feet once again, letting the towel fall from her body. Staring at her reflection in the wavy mirror across the room, she thought it was hopeless. No wonder Kane resisted her. Her eyes were too big for her face, her hair straggly, her body completely lacking in the curve department. In her dreams, Kane liked her exactly as she was. In her dreams, he loved her. Silly, little girl dreams.

She cracked a window, slipped a nightgown over her head and set about freshening the room up a little. She didn't know where Kane was. He hadn't come inside, and a peek out the window was all it took to let her know that he was no longer sitting on the fence, staring at his mountains. Feeling more dejected than she had in a long, long time, she crawled into bed shortly after eleven.

Sometime later, the outer door creaked open. Kane's footsteps sounded in the kitchen, and then in the hall, pausing outside her door. Josie held perfectly still, fingers crossed, hoping and praying he would turn the handle and come inside. After what seemed like forever, his footsteps faded away. Disappointed, she rolled to her side and closed her eyes.

She'd dreamed about Kane often these past two weeks. In her dreams, he called her name in the middle of the night, and came to her, bold and rugged.

Her thoughts drifted, sleep slowly claiming her. She thought she heard the door open and the bed creak. Hmm. She realized she was dreaming again. In her dream, Kane was sitting on the edge of the bed, leaning over her. The sky was hazy outside her window, the moon a tiny sliver in the sky, the only sound that of Kane's huskily drawn breath and his masculine sound of pleasure. Josie tried to open her eyes, but couldn't. Moaning softly, she glided one bare knee down Kane's muscled leg.

"What the…"

The voice carried away on a groan of pleasure, and then those big, work-roughened hands were everywhere, familiar yet different, sliding across her shoulder, gliding down to her waist, over her hip. His right arm was much stronger. But of course it was. She was dreaming, and in her dreams he was always as strong as Hercules and the most romantic man who had ever lived. On second thought, she didn't want to wake up.

Lips nuzzled her neck, her jaw, the sensitive skin below her ear. "You're a present I wasn't expecting, but oh, it's good to be home," that familiar yet different voice murmured against her skin. His breath was hot and moist; his mustache tickled her skin.

Josie's eyes popped open. Everything else went perfectly still.

Mustache? Kane didn't have a mustache.

She was fully awake now, and fully panicked. *Oh-my-God!* This was no dream. Someone was in her bed. Someone who wasn't Kane.

She leaped to the floor and let loose a bloodcurdling scream.

Chapter Seven

Footsteps thundered down the hall. Wood splintered and Kane burst into the room, pistol drawn. The door banged against the wall, the light from the hall throwing his shadow across the floor. Josie wanted to run to him, to hide behind him, but she couldn't seem to move.

She glanced at the other man. His hands were in the air, his eyes squinting against the sudden burst of light. "For crying out loud, Kane. Don't shoot. It's only me!"

"Trace!"

Trace? Josie felt as if she was watching a Ping-Pong match.

"What the hell are you doing here?"

"I live here," the man sputtered, lowering his hands. "Or at least I used to. On second thought, if you're going to shoot me, get it over with. Who's the girl?"

Suddenly two pairs of eyes were trained on Josie. Kane looked big and intimidating and strong. It took a moment for her to realize he was naked. Now that she was alert and coherent, she noticed that Trace, if that's who he was, was naked, too.

She cast a sweeping glance over each of them—oh, my!—mustache or not, there was no mistaking the family resemblance. Trying to avert her eyes before her cheeks could flame and give her away, she fixed her gaze on the floor. Josie Slater, you're a wicked, wicked woman.

Biting her lip to keep from smiling, she glanced across the room at Kane's younger brother. "You're Trace?" she asked, doing her level best to keep her eyes trained above his shoulders.

With a wink a gentleman would never get away with, Trace Slater said, "It seems a little late to shake your hand, doesn't it?"

Josie would have had an easier time trying to stop a speeding freight train than hiding the grin that was sliding across her face. "Yes, I suppose it is a little late for that. I'm Josephine Slater—Josie to my friends, and in your case, family—I'm your new sister-in-law."

"My new—" Trace's head jerked around, his surprise giving way to honest concern the instant he noticed the injury on Kane's shoulder. "What happened to you?"

Kane shrugged. "I got in the way of a stray bullet."

"You don't say. A gunshot wound and a new wife. Now I know why Gwen always gives me hell for not calling more often. Are you going to live?"

"For now," Kane answered.

Although Trace appeared more amused than uncomfortable about the fact that he was standing—as naked as the day he was born—in a semi-lit room with a woman he'd just met, he pulled on his jeans and deftly fastened the front closure. As if thoroughly enjoying Kane's thunderous expression, the younger man reached for his shoes and shirt with one hand and his ratty duffel bag with the other. "I think I'll move my butt and my gear over to Spence's place tonight.''

"You do that," Kane said as Trace backed from the room.

"It was nice to make your acquaintance," Josie called.

Trace's smile turned beguiling beneath his mustache. ''The pleasure was almost all mine.''

Josie laughed out loud. Kane didn't appear to think it was funny. When the outer door slammed, alerting them to Trace's departure, Kane glared at her as if she was somehow responsible for his sudden black mood. "What the hell did he mean by that?''

She knew better than to antagonize a man when he was in the throes of a dark mood, but doggone it, she wouldn't cower, either. Pushing her hair out of her face and the thin strap of her nightgown back up on her shoulder, she raised her chin a notch and said, ''He's *your* brother.''

Kane heaved a sigh and lowered the pistol to his side.

Josie sauntered closer, her heart brimming with emotion, because it seemed her virtue wasn't the only thing safe with this man. She stopped within touching distance, and lightly skimmed her fingers across his shoulder. ''You're going to have a bruise in the morning, and I'm not sure the door will ever be the same.''

When he didn't answer, she glanced up at him, and found him staring at her mouth. Her lips parted, a tender feeling spreading through her. She was alone in the semidarkness with her husband who just happened to have nothing on. But, alas, a promise was a promise. Kane was going to have to be the one to make the next move, and he appeared frozen in time.

"Well," she whispered, for lack of anything else to say. ''It's been an interesting night, hasn't it?''

Kane took a ragged breath. The air was scented of pine

and the first bluebells of the season. It stirred a distant memory, but he couldn't quite put his finger on what the memory was. Josie was looking up at him, her pupils dilated in the near darkness, so that only a ring of gray encircled them. Something shifted in his chest, his tension draining away. Shaking his head slightly, he said, "That's some scream you've got."

Her gray eyes looked sleepy and mellow as she said, "I guess the first thing I should do is thank you for coming to my rescue."

Before he could ask about the second thing, her lips touched his, tenderly and so damn sweetly he almost cried out like a little boy in need of comfort. It rekindled old feelings deep inside him, old emotions and sentiments he thought he'd forgotten.

Too soon, she drew away. He felt himself being propelled toward the door. The next thing he knew, she was closing it an inch at a time. Peeking through the narrow opening, she said, "You don't make it easy for a girl to keep her promise not to seduce you. Tell me something, Kane. Have you ever worn a mustache?"

His eyes narrowed suspiciously. "Just what did you and my brother do?"

Josie closed the door another inch, the hinges creaking due to Kane's dramatic entrance a few minutes earlier. Smiling ruefully, she said, "Quite a little more than I normally do with a man I don't know, that's for sure. Don't worry, Kane. What I did, I thought I was doing with you. Good night."

Kane staggered backward, the hair on the back of his neck standing on end as if he'd come too close to an electric fence.

What the hell had she meant by that? Had she kissed Trace or hadn't she? Had he touched her?

For crying out loud, Trace Slater was a lady-killer from way back. He probably hadn't thought a thing of finding a willing woman in his bed. Oh, he would have touched her, all right. He would have done whatever she let him do.

Kane slammed into his own room. Just how willing had Josie been? She'd said that whatever she'd done, she'd thought she'd been doing with him. She'd been plenty willing up in that mountain cabin, and a few times since.

He stuffed his gun into its holster and jerked around, the sudden movement reminding him of his injury. He swore at the pain slicing through him. He swore at his interrupted sleep, and at the desire coursing through him. He stomped out to the kitchen to make himself a sandwich, and cussed out the knife he dropped. He picked up the ball he was supposed to use to exercise his hand, only to drop it in frustration. He was still cussing when he went back to his room.

Josie heard Kane slamming through the house. As far as she could tell, he'd sputtered and cussed about everybody and everything. She smiled into the darkness. Finally she was getting a reaction from him. It wasn't the reaction she'd wanted, but it was a reaction just the same. Maybe she was making progress, after all.

She'd set out to keep him off balance. In the process, she was learning a little something about the man she'd married. He had a temper, but he had integrity, too. She'd spent the last several days trying to get him to open up to her. Big and brooding, he wasn't an easy man to know. He wasn't an easy man, period. She rolled her eyes in the darkness at that understatement.

She sensed sadness buried deep inside him. It was at the heart of what he did for a living and why he'd been alone for so long. She didn't understand it, but she wanted to ease it so he could heal. She thought a good place to start would have been in bed. The big oaf insisted they sleep in separate rooms. He wanted her. She was more certain of that every day. Whether he admitted it or not, he needed her, too. As soon as he stopped being so stubborn, they could both have what they needed.

One of these days, she told herself, pulling the sheet around her neck and closing her eyes, Kane was going to stop fighting his needs and open his arms and his heart to her. Something told her that day wasn't far away.

"Here you go, Kane," Gwen said, passing an oval platter to the end of the table. "I made this steak especially for you."

"Barely warm and bloody in the middle," Spence added, passing the platter on.

Trace made a *mooing* sound and asked Kane when he'd started eating his steaks without the tail. Even six-year-old Mallory and four-year-old Melissa caught their uncle's humor and giggled behind their hands. Everyone else laughed outright.

Josie had never heard so much noise in this house. As far as she was concerned, noise and laughter were good things. They added to her feelings that the problems she was having with Kane were going to work out, which in turn sent a burgeoning sense of excitement all the way through her.

Twenty-nine and well-traveled, Trace Slater had regaled them with stories about the silver he'd found in an unmarked mine in the mountains in Colorado. He claimed that was where his next adventure lay. Unfortunately he couldn't remember which mine had held the treasure. Josie wasn't certain how much of what he said was truth and how much was Irish bull, but she had to admit that he brought a lot of life into this family. The little girls flocked around him, begging for attention, making it obvious that he was the family favorite.

"You're puttin' on a little weight, aren't you, Gwen?" he asked while she served dessert.

"Mommy's going to have a baby," four-year-old Melissa stated proudly, as if Trace hadn't noticed.

Trace winked at his niece. "You know, Spence," he said under his breath. "Scientists have figured out what causes that."

Even Kane had smiled at that one.

When everyone had had their fill of thick steaks, mashed potatoes and gravy, homemade rolls and cherry pie, Gwen instructed the men to carry their dishes into the kitchen. Stacking everything in the sink, she turned on the radio and took Spence's hand. "Come on, sweetheart," she said, leading the way out to the dining room. "Let's dance."

By now everyone knew that Trace was going to say something to the effect that Gwen was bigger than a barn and in no shape for dancing. Slapping him on the back on his way by, Spence cut his brother off. "Give me a little warning before you get married so you and I can have a long talk about how to treat women."

"I know how to treat women. Don't I, Josie?"

Josie was so busy watching Gwen and Spence dance cheek to cheek that she didn't notice Kane's eyes narrow and his lips form a thin line. No matter what Trace implied to the contrary, Gwen was beautiful, the way brides and angels were beautiful. Her smile was warm and serene, her hair the color of fresh-ground coffee, her face as lively as her personality. Spence looked a lot like Kane and Trace. His hair was sandy brown, his shoulders broad, his body lean, his face shaped by masculine planes and interesting hollows. He could be as quiet and brooding as Kane, but he held Gwen as if he knew a secret his brothers had yet to figure out.

Josie crossed her hands over her heart and tipped her head slightly. Tears glistened on her lashes and made her throat feel thick. She hadn't seen that kind of love since before her mama had died. Yearning washed over her, and suddenly she wanted to be held in Kane's arms and loved like that. "Dance with me?" she whispered.

"We should go."

His stormy expression took her by surprise. "Go?" she asked, flinching slightly at the chill that had grown between them out of nowhere.

"Go?" Trace echoed, coming up behind Kane. "You can't go. The night's still young."

Glancing from one to the other, Josie said, "Just one dance, Kane?"

"I don't want to dance, dammit."

The harsh tone of Kane's voice raised Josie's hackles. Since when had the world revolved around what he wanted to do?

She had wishes and needs, too, didn't she? Turning to his younger brother, she said, "How about you, Trace? Do you feel like dancing?"

Trace held up both hands in a show of innocence. "I can't dance."

Josie reached for Trace's hand. "Put on your dancing shoes, because this is your lucky day."

"Honey," he said, letting her lead him to the center of the floor. "That's what I thought last night."

Kane scowled. As Josie's laughter blended with Trace's, he groped blindly for a pack of cigarettes. Great, he'd left them in his other shirt. He clenched his teeth and squeezed his fingers into fists at his side. The tension in his gut only coiled tighter.

By now, Josie had given Trace a quick lesson, and the two of them were moving stiffly across the floor. Kane wanted to bite glass. Damn slow song, anyway.

This was crazy. He trusted his brothers with his life. Trace was all talk, and Kane knew it. Why then, did he feel more on edge with every passing second?

So Josie and Trace were dancing? So what? So Josie was talking and laughing. Josie was always talking and laughing. Trace may have been a lady-killer from way back, but he was no better at dancing than Kane was. The number of times he stepped on Josie's toes proved it. Logically Kane knew Trace was only having fun. Kane was in no mood to listen to logic. Doing an about-face, he turned on his heel and let the screen door bang shut behind him.

The dancing came to an abrupt end. "Uh-oh," Trace said.

"Uh-oh," Mallory echoed.

"Uncle Kane's mad again," Melissa declared.

Josie's hands went to her hips. "Now what?"

Without waiting for an answer, she strode out the door and hurried after Kane. He was halfway to the bunkhouse when she caught up with him.

"Hold it right there, mister."

He didn't hold it right there. He didn't even slow down.

"Have a heart, Kane," she sputtered, traipsing after him. "At least tell me what's wrong."

He stopped so suddenly she nearly ran into him. "I told you, dammit. I don't have a heart."

Josie felt as if she was standing at a fork in the road beneath a thick cloud of swirling fog high in her mountain. One direction led to Kane's heart, the other to destruction. Since she couldn't see her way, she had to rely on her other senses. Slowly she placed one hand on his chest and raised her eyes to his. "You have a heart, Kane. I can feel it beating."

"You know what I mean."

"No," she said, her voice rising. "I don't know what you mean. How could I? You don't talk to me. You rarely look at me. You won't even sleep with me."

"Maybe you should talk to Trace about that. He could probably help you out."

That was a nasty thing to say, but she was beginning to realize that Kane could be nasty when it suited him. "Trace? Trace?" she sputtered, at a complete and utter loss for anything else to say. "Is that what this is all about?"

"Why don't you tell me!" he replied snidely. "You two seemed pretty cozy a few minutes ago."

Josie's stomach churned with frustration. She raised her chin and gritted her teeth. "I resent that insinuation. As long as I'm on the subject, I resent your entire attitude toward me."

His stare drilled into her. "What did you expect?"

"What did I—" the churning in Josie's stomach gave way like a volcanic eruption. "That does it." She accented every word with a sharp poke in his chest. "Put up your dukes, Slater. Now."

"Put up my—"

She poked him in the chest again. "That's right. Your dukes. You're itching for a fight, aren't you? Well, come on. We'll fight to the finish. Loser concedes defeat."

Fists raised, she glared at him.

Kane's eyes narrowed. "Cut it out, Josie."

"Why should I?"

He jumped back in the nick of time, the breeze from her fist the only thing grazing his chin.

"I mean it, Josie."

"What do you mean?" Another punch sailed out of the blue. This one came even closer than the first one.

He turned and slipped through the bunkhouse door. Josie followed close behind. Grabbing him by the arm, she stopped his forward motion, landing a hard jab in the middle of his stomach.

Oomph. He'd felt that one. "I don't want to fight with you, dammit."

"You don't want to fight with me."

"No, I don't." He dodged her next blow.

"You don't want to dance with me."

Realizing that she wasn't expecting a reply, he managed to stop her right fist with his left hand.

"You don't want to talk to me."

Her actions became more frenzied, as if she was working up to a full-scale war.

"You don't want to make love with me."

"Josie." He moved backward, breathing hard in his efforts to ward off more blows. "Ouch." He grasped her wrists in his hands and held them fast.

"Let go of me and fight like a man."

Her right hand slipped out of his grasp. In an effort to keep her from pummeling him again, he wrapped his arms around her body and pulled her hard against him. "I am a man, dammit, and I won't hit a woman."

"At least you admit that I'm a woman."

She writhed against him, trying to get free. Kane held her tighter. He anticipated the knee she tried to bring up, and repositioned her so she couldn't hurt him.

"Kane, let me go."

His hold didn't loosen, but it changed subtly. He moved against her, rolling his hips into hers. She stopped fighting, and she held perfectly still.

Josie knew her eyes were wide and her mouth was open.

She couldn't help her surprise. She wasn't certain of the exact moment the atmosphere had changed. One minute she'd been pushing away from the hard angles and planes of Kane's body, and the next she'd been molded to them. Beneath her hand, his heart beat an erratic rhythm. Bit by bit, the fight drained out of her. She'd read somewhere that what a person needed wasn't a clear plan, but a clear intent. She doubted Kane had intended to respond to her in this manner, but Josie didn't intend to pass up such a glorious opportunity.

Raising up on tiptoe, she whispered, "I'm sorry I hit you. I think I know what's ailing you. It's ailing me, too. We're both frustrated, that's all."

She kissed his neck, slowly working her way down the skin bared with every button she unfastened. "We're married, Kane, and married people don't have to be this frustrated. I lie awake nights pining after you. I've saved myself for twenty-three years, and I don't want to wait any longer. You don't want to wait any longer, either, do you?"

Kane turned his head in time to catch a glimpse of his shirt sailing to the floor. Her fingers moved on to the buckle on his belt. He was pretty sure she was talking, although it was difficult to hear through the ringing in his ears. When she moved on to the front closure on his jeans, he closed his eyes and concentrated on the passion tearing through him. He took one slow breath, and then another. He knew he should fight it, but when her hand dipped inside the low-slung waistband of his jeans, passion took up residence where his anger and determination had been.

The woman played dirty, but she was right about his frustration, and she was right about what they needed to do about it. It was so like Josie to point it out to him. It was so like her to pick a fistfight with someone twice her size, and then talk the entire time she was undressing him.

Because that's what she was doing. Talking *and* undressing him. "I saw a stray cat in the barn last night. After a lot of searching, I found where she'd hidden her kittens. I'd really like to bring one inside, if it's all right with you."

His zipper rasped as she lowered it. "Did you know that a group of domestic cats is called a clowder? That's an old-fashioned word for clutter."

"Josie."

"I read that somewhere. A group of lions is called a pride. I don't know why, but that kind of information stays in my brain."

She looked up at him, her gaze emotion-filled and uncertain, her fingers fluttering beneath his. Placing his hand over her breast, he felt her heart flutter, as well. And he knew her bravado was only an act. This woman who had saved his life and had seemed certain of her rightful place in the world wasn't certain at all.

"Josie," he said again, touching a finger to her cheek.

Her eyelashes lowered and lifted again, accenting her uncertainty, her longing. It was as if she knew he could reject her, yet she was placing the power in his hands. Suddenly Kane didn't want to hurt her. He wanted to touch her, and give her what she was asking for.

Night was falling, shadows stealing into corners, filling the old bunkhouse with a hazy intimacy. Kane glided his fingertip over her lips, down to the delicate hollow in her neck where her pulse was beating fast. "There's nothing to be afraid of, Josie. Making love is like dancing. It's all about leading and following, about trust and consent."

The quiver on her lips might have been a smile. It struck a vibrant chord inside him, making him feel big and strong and tender at the same time. Keeping his voice low and his touch gentle, he worked the buttons down the front of her knit shirt free.

"Passion has a rhythm," he murmured, covering her breasts with his hands. "A pulse all its own. You move with it. Not against it. Like this. Do you feel that?"

Josie closed her eyes dreamily. Oh, my! She felt that all right. "Kane?" she whispered. "Do you think we could stop talking now?"

His laughter sounded rusty, husky, and sent a curious swooping to Josie's insides. She felt herself being lifted, carried to his room. With his shirt off and hers open, skin glided over skin as he lowered her feet to the floor. He kissed her again, and helped her out of her knit shirt. Her shoes came next, and then her belt. When she was wearing only the new panties she'd purchased in Butternut earlier that day, she tugged Kane down next to her and deftly straddled his lap, wiggling until she found what she'd been searching for.

Kane heard the rumble of his moan deep in his own throat, but he was more aware of the way Josie was shifting closer to the part of him burning with need. With a hand on either side of her narrow hips, he brought her hard against him. Her eyes popped open, and he swore he'd never seen such a look of rapture on any woman's face. She may have been a virgin, but she was very sensuous, very responsive—she shifted on his lap—not to mention an extremely fast learner.

She brought her hands to his shoulders and wavered him a soft, womanly smile. And then she leaned closer, her breath hot on his neck, her kisses wet on his skin. He couldn't remember the last time he'd been so aroused. Hell, he couldn't remember if he'd ever been so aroused. He wanted to press her into the mattress and bury himself inside her, without warning, without the prelude of so much as another kiss. But this would be her first time, and he had to be as gentle as possible.

She climbed off his lap and lithely whisked her panties from her body. "Hurry, Kane," she said, "Don't make me wait any longer."

"Easy," he said, shedding his remaining clothes. "We have all night."

"I don't want you to take it easy. I want…" Her voice trailed away. "You know what I want."

Kane took a moment to appreciate Josie's nakedness. Her lips were swollen, her eyes soft looking, her arms open in invitation. Her skin was a pale color of cream, her breasts pert and pink and perfect. She may have been slender, but her hips had a womanly flare, her thighs soft and supple looking. He'd spent night after night reliving what had almost happened in that mountain cabin, night after night imagining finishing what they'd started. Josie had been willing then. Now, she was literally trembling with anticipation. It was going to make going slow mighty difficult, but it was going to make completion damned incredible.

Need took on an identity of its own within him. Laying down beside her, he covered her legs with one of his, gliding his hand down her side, kneading and molding her soft flesh. Her body was pliant and smooth, yet strong in a way that filled him with wonder. It was magic. He covered her breasts with his hands, toyed with them with his fingers and finally took each, in turn, into his mouth. She writhed and moaned. And then she reached down, her fingertips working their own brand of magic on his body. It was all he could do to hold on to the last of his control. She responded to his every touch, opening her mouth beneath his kiss, holding his head, his shoulders, gliding her hands along his sensitized skin.

Josie had been dreaming of this for weeks. She wanted this more than she'd ever wanted anything in her life. Still, one corner of her mind held a hint of nervousness. Every time Kane touched her in that amazing way, sensation took over, and her nerves receded a little further. She loved this man, her husband. She wanted this to be as special for him as it was for her. Letting her instincts guide her, she kissed him full on the mouth, rolling onto her back, bringing him on top of her. Her breath caught in her throat at the feel of him against her most sensitive flesh.

Kane's need was strong, his restraint waning. He pressed himself against her, feeling her give in places that had never given before. Sweat broke out on his brow in his effort to be gentle.

Beneath him, Josie opened her eyes. He tried to read her expression, trying to determine if her eyes had darkened in pain, or maybe in fear. When he moved another inch, her eyes widened. The next thing he knew, the little tart smiled. The last shred of Kane's control evaporated. Grasping her hips, he buried himself inside her, finishing what he'd started up in the mountain cabin.

Josie didn't deny the discomfort. She didn't deny the way her body started to quake with sensation, either. She cried Kane's name, and he covered her mouth with his, capturing her gasp in his kiss. Her breasts tingled against his chest, her hips rising to meet his. Her senses reeled, and the most amazing thing began to happen where those butterfly wings had been.

Oh my, oh my, oh my!

Kane seemed to be waiting for something, his face contorting as if in pain. When she cried out in release, his eyes closed, his expression changing to one of pure pleasure. He increased the tempo of his movements, the quaking in her body increasing, quieting, only to flare again. Groaning her name, he followed her to a place that seemed to be made for them alone.

She surfaced to the sound of Kane's ragged breathing,

smiling in the gathering darkness at the way he suddenly became so careful of her. She kissed his shoulder, thinking it was a little late to be careful.

If Josie would have known it would be like this, she wouldn't have waited so long. That wasn't true, she thought to herself. It wasn't sex she'd been waiting for. It was Kane.

Ah, Kane. What he'd done to her, with her, had been incredible. She knew she would have to get up eventually. She even admitted that she was a little apprehensive as to what she would discover once she'd closed the bathroom door behind her. But right now, she didn't want to break the spell of intimacy enveloping them. So she simply snuggled against his side. And she sighed.

Kane drifted back to earth in layers. His heart was still beating heavily, but his breathing was growing more even, and his eyes refused to remain open. His entire body felt warm and languid. Ah, sex. There was nothing else like it on earth, nothing more stimulating, invigorating, stress-relieving.

He couldn't take all the credit. Josie had been pretty damn incredible, trembling and writhing, giving and taking, tending to his needs, reacting to his touch. She'd spurred him on, and made him forget everything except the pleasure between a man and a woman. Stroking his hand over her hair, he wondered if he'd hurt her. He opened his mouth to ask, but her silence kept him still.

Josie was never this quiet.

He peered down at her, trying to see her clearly in the darkness. He might have been imagining the smile on her lips, but he wasn't imagining the steady rise and fall of her chest or the way her eyes were closed. Josie was sound asleep.

The tender feelings pushing against Kane's chest were almost painful. He took a deep breath. Closing his eyes, his thoughts began to drift. Hmm. What was that scent? Whatever it was, he hadn't smelled it in a long, long time. It seemed fitting, because he hadn't felt this way in a long time, either.

Being careful not to jostle Josie, he pulled a quilt up around them. Moments before sleep claimed him, he took another breath. Bluebells. They'd been Maggie's favorite flower.

Kane's eyes opened, his thoughts stacking up, one on top of the other. He stared at the ceiling for a long time, waiting for his stomach to unclench. Maggie, with her dark hair and gentle smile had been nothing like Josie. Nothing.

After a long pause, during which he fought for self-control, he slid out of bed and pulled on his clothes and boots. At the last minute he reached for his holster. Heart chugging, thoughts careening, he left his bedroom without a backward glance.

Chapter Eight

Early-morning sunlight shimmered, golden, on the other side of Josie's closed eyelids. Hovering between sleep and wakefulness, she stretched, the stiffness and soreness in her body reminding her of last night. A smile found its way to her lips. Making love had been incredible. Kane had been incredible. She wondered what he would say if she asked him to do it again. He wouldn't mind, would he? Men on television never minded. She'd read somewhere that the love scenes on television and in the movies were carefully choreographed to achieve the highest possible impact and effect on an audience. What Kane and she had done last night hadn't been planned, let alone choreographed, and yet it had a profound effect and impact on her.

The mere thought of it broadened her smile. She moved her foot to the center of the bed, slowly inching it onto Kane's side. Her toes came uncovered, but they didn't come into contact with Kane's legs. Deciding he must be the type who slept on the very edge of the bed, she rolled to her side and opened her eyes.

Kane's side of the bed was empty.

Listening intently, she sat up, her smile sliding away. Other than early-morning songbirds chirping outside the window, the house was silent. She sniffed the air for the telltale scent of the bacon and eggs Kane insisted upon fixing himself every morning. Only the subtle scent of wildflowers carried to her nostrils.

She glanced around the room. The clothes and boots he'd been wearing last night were gone. It was barely six a.m. Too early for Kane to be out on the range. Too early for him to be up, period. For some reason, her gaze rested on a peg near the door where he kept his gun and holster. The peg was empty.

A disturbing sense of unease settled over her as she slipped from the bed, worry overriding the tenderness in her body. After pulling on her robe, she checked the spare room and the sofa. Both were empty. Where could he be?

Peering out the window, she relived Kane's touch, his kiss, and how, much later, she'd snuggled into his side, sated and sleepy and secure in the belief that she was slowly finding a way into his heart. Half in anticipation, half in dread, she padded out to the kitchen. Except for the note lying on the table, the room was exactly as she'd left it last night.

Intuition told her she wasn't going to like what the note said. Just as she suspected, Kane's scrawl was barely legible, the note brief and to the point. He'd gone bounty hunting. He didn't know when he would be back.

Josie sank into a nearby chair. He'd been half-frozen and bleeding when he'd stumbled into her mountain cabin that first time. She'd seen him in action again two nights ago when he'd busted through her door, pistol drawn. The thought of him tailing hardened criminals who had everything to lose left a bad taste in her mouth, a bad feeling in the pit of her stomach. Why would a man like Kane take chances like that? He'd said growing old didn't run in his family. If he died on a bounty hunt, it wouldn't be of natural causes. Fear squeezed like a fist around Josie's windpipe. Why would Kane tempt fate? And why now, after they'd finally made love?

Refusing to give in to the panic and apprehension sweeping over her, she jumped to her feet and sputtered, "Kane Slater, if you make me a widow before I have a chance to give you a piece of my mind, I'll never forgive you. You come home and face the music. You hear me?"

Spinning around, she traipsed into the bathroom. Ornery, thickheaded, stubborn man.

Josie heard a pickup truck pull into the driveway, but she'd be darned if she'd give in to the need to see if it was the ornery, thickheaded stubborn man she'd married.

She'd lost track of how many times she'd watched the road for his return these past five days. Probably about the same number of times she'd cussed him out under her breath. There had been concern in Gwen's eyes when Josie had told her what Kane had done, but not surprise. Trace and Spence had each called their brother a name or two, but they'd had no words of advice for Josie. She'd given herself plenty of advice. Forget him. Leave him. Throttle him.

She loved him. That made forgetting him and leaving him out of the question. But throttling him was still an option.

She heard the truck door slam, followed a few seconds later by the banging of the bunkhouse door. Feeling spiteful, she started the circular saw. Noise rent the air, sawdust spraying onto the old plank floor. Setting the saw to one side of the makeshift workbench moments later, she glanced over her shoulder, straight into Kane's light brown eyes.

She paused, at a complete and utter loss for something to say.

He ambled closer, all cowboy brawn and masculine appeal. "I wondered if I'd find you in here."

His voice was entirely too deep, his gaze far too steady. The man was a sight for sore eyes, darn it all, from his sandy brown hair all the way down to the scuffed toes of his worn cowboy boots. This was the first time she'd seen him since she'd fallen asleep curled next to him. Shoring her heart against the renewed hurt winding through her, she tossed her hair over her shoulder and declared, "Well, looky what the cat dragged in."

He stopped in his tracks near the door, her traitorous heart stopping right along with him. That did it. From now on, she absolutely, positively forbade herself to respond to the ruggedness of his features or the huskiness in his voice.

"What? No bullet holes?"

"You almost sound disappointed."

She took a sudden interest in the sawdust clinging to her long denim skirt, in the nails and straight-edge in front of her and the wood strewn all around, but she did nothing to further the conversation. Why should she? He was the one who'd left without so much as a wham, bam, thank you, ma'am.

"You're mad."

Darned right she was mad. Mad at herself for being glad to see him and mad at him for making her glad. "Who, me? Whatever gave you that idea?" She cast him a look that spoke volumes then deftly reached for the saw.

Kane settled his hands on his hips and calmly assessed the situation. He'd spent the better part of the past five days in the shadows, and had had plenty of time to wonder about

Josie's reaction to his leaving and his eventual return. He hadn't been able to picture her weeping, and although he wasn't surprised by her anger, he didn't know how she did it, how she exuded so much vitality and sass with a simple quirk of her brow and jerk of her chin.

He hitched a finger through his belt loop, and contemplated striding closer. Deciding it would be safer to wait until after she turned off the saw, he strode to the shelves containing more than a dozen finished birdhouses. Upon closer inspection, he decided birdhouses was too broad a term for the small structures she'd built. Why, she'd constructed a whole bird town and had moved on to country structures. He wondered where she got her ideas. Hell, where had she gotten her talent?

When she turned off the saw, he said, "There's a lot more to you than your constant chatter, isn't there? I don't believe I've ever seen a bird *barn*."

Josie tapped a nail into the roof she was working on. Keeping her tone cool and impersonal, she said, "Your regard for me is staggering, but you're probably right about my birdhouses. I don't suppose there are a lot of bird *barns* in the world."

He turned slowly. "How have you been, Josie?"

Kane noticed she didn't rush right in with an answer. In fact, she didn't answer his question at all.

"Back in Tennessee," she said, as if he hadn't spoken, "I spent more time talkin' to folks than building birdhouses. Montana ain't—isn't—exactly crawling with people to talk to."

He took a few steps closer, lulled by the cool, clear tone of her voice.

"Don't get me wrong," she said, reaching for another nail. "Gwen, at least, has been great. But she's got two little ones to care for and books to keep and a house to run.

I decided I'd better find something to do to keep myself busy, so I asked her for directions to the nearest lumber company or sawmill where I could buy the supplies I needed to build more birdhouses. Gwen must have told Spence, because he showed up at the bunkhouse door, hat in hand, and told me I could have any wood I could salvage from that old shed that's falling down at the end of the lane. I took one look at the aged boards and weathered roof and got so excited I almost forgot how mad I was at you."

Kane stopped on the other side of her makeshift workbench. He'd been feeling guilty about the way he'd left her five days ago. Running his fingers through his hair, all he could think to say was, "I had my reasons for leaving like I did, but I didn't do it to make you angry."

The only indication she gave that she'd heard him was the slight stilling of her fingertips. She recovered almost immediately, picking up the conversation where she'd left off. "Anyway, Trace hooked one end of a rope to the shed and the other end to the bumper of the Jeep then took off like a bat out of you know where. The Jeep's a little worse for wear, but that old building folded up like a house of cards. He helped me tear down one wall before he left."

"Trace cleared out again?"

She chose that moment to look his way. "The same as you. Without so much as a word or a wave goodbye."

"It's what I do, Josie."

Up close, he could see the sawdust in her hair. Her mouth was set, but far back in her eyes, hurt glittered like tears. Damn. He didn't like hurting people. That was why he kept to himself. It was why he'd stopped in to see the attorney on his way through Butte again, too. Going to bed with Josie had been a mistake, a once-in-a-lifetime aberration. It wasn't like him to allow himself to be carried away by the moment. He'd given it a lot of thought, and the only

explanation he could come up with was the fact that he'd
felt different since the moment he'd opened his eyes in that
mountain cabin. Of course he felt different. Coming that
close to death would have a life-altering effect on anyone.
He was getting stronger every day. As soon as those divorce papers arrived his life would go on the way it had
been before.

"So," she asked after a long stretch of silence. "Did
you get your man?"

Kane nodded. "The fugitive is behind bars, and I never
even had to draw my gun. Hell, I never even worked up a
sweat."

"You don't sound very happy about it."

He didn't know why her observation rankled. "I spent
the better part of the past five days huddled in my truck
surrounded by stale smoke and fast-food wrappers, waiting
for the bail hopper to make his move. It was boring as hell,
but until my shoulder is completely healed, I'm going to
have to put up with the easy cases. And as far as being
happy goes, I don't do it for the sake of my happiness."

"You sure don't do it for your health."

He was pretty sure she only turned on the saw out of
spite. He waited for her to finish making the cut before
saying, "Bounty hunters don't make good husbands. That's
why I suggested the annulment."

She skirted the edge of the work station with the ease
and grace of a dancer. Meeting his gaze, she said, "It's a
little too late for that now, Kane."

He had every intention of sputtering, *Do you think I
don't know that?* But his gaze got stuck on her lower lip,
and he ended up swallowing, instead. He found himself
studying her profile, the slender column of her neck, the
hollow little ridge below her collarbone visible at the edge
of the V neckline of her pale blue shirt. It had been almost

a week since he'd pressed his lips to that soft patch of skin. Damn, he wanted to kiss her there—and elsewhere—again.

Josie had every intention of holding on to her anger, but she glanced up, and found Kane watching her. Silence stretched between them, the air filling with waiting, the heat in his eyes stoking a gently growing fire. Her anger slipped out of her like water through a sieve.

His fingers flexed at his side as if he wanted to reach out to her, but couldn't. She had nothing on which to gauge her next move, no past experience or knowledge of what to do at a time like this. She only knew he seemed to need to kiss her, and touch her. There were a lot of things she didn't understand about Kane, but she understood his need, because she had a similar need for him.

She skirted the makeshift workbench, gliding to a stop mere inches from him. "I don't want to argue, Kane. I don't think you do, either. That's good, because we don't have to argue. There's something else we can do, instead."

Kane felt a chugging in his heart, and heard a roaring din in his ears. He considered himself a logical, reasonable man, but there was nothing logical or reasonable about the current racing through him. He wasn't accustomed to this sudden surge of desire in the middle of the day. He sure as hell wasn't accustomed to doing something about it. As he watched her come closer, he knew that was exactly what he wanted to do.

Possibilities squeezed into his chest, leaving him warm and wanting in both body and spirit. He was almost thankful when the air whooshed out of him. It forced him to take a deep breath, and allowed him to shove the wanting to some far corner of his brain and concentrate on getting Josie out of her clothes.

Her shirt came off with ease. She toed out of her shoes, then moved to unfasten his belt. He pushed her hands aside.

"You don't want me to help?" she asked, brave for somebody who was only one lovemaking session away from being a virgin.

He shook his head, his answer escaping on a low growl. "This isn't about want. *This* is all about need."

Heart jolting, pulse pounding, Josie stood back while Kane unbuttoned his shirt, unfastened the top closure on his jeans and deftly lowered the zipper. Perhaps he was right and need was all that was between them. She'd known of lesser things binding a man and woman. She wasn't ashamed of this need. It connected them on a soul-deep level. Her need for him, and his for her, the need to hold and to be held, the need to kiss and express emotions, to touch and caress and respond.

Need was better than nothing. It was better than loneliness and sleeping alone. It wasn't love, but for now, it was enough.

Josie stood before Kane, her feet bare, the chill in the April afternoon raising goose bumps on her upper body. She felt his gaze on her shoulders, her breasts. Although it required all the courage she possessed, she raised her eyes to his. The look on his face held her perfectly still. She wanted to take his face between her hands, and kiss each cheek, to murmur sweet nothings along the hard line of his jaw, the corner of his mouth. She wished there was a pile of loose straw tucked in a corner somewhere, but this was an old tack room; other than a bench covered with old stirrups and horseshoes, there was only the hard plank floor.

"There's no place to lie down," she whispered.

Taking her hand as if leading her into a waltz, he said, "We don't need a place to lie down."

We don't? she thought, not fully understanding. As he slowly drew her closer, she reminded herself that making love wasn't about understanding. It was about trust and consent and need. And Kane needed her. ''What if someone sees us?'' she asked.

Kane shook his head. ''The girls never venture out here. Too many dark corners and shadows. There's no one here, but you. And me.''

Seeing the haggard look of a man who had used up all but the last shred of his control, she opened her arms to him. He lifted her off her feet so fast she gasped. Five days ago he'd tried to be careful and take things slow. Today, he seemed beyond either of those things. His lips covered hers, his hands lifting her higher, his movements brisk and impatient as he pushed her skirt up and her panties aside.

Her eyes popped open, her breath catching in her throat. Since he seemed to know what he was doing, she let him lead her into the most intimate dance in the world.

Late-afternoon sunlight slanted through the lone window high in the rafters. The rest of the room was cast in shadow, the scent of sawdust and barn wood heavy on the air. In the books Josie read, starlight and roses were the stuff romance was made of. The sound of Kane's voice as he whispered her name, the touch of his hands, the feel of his heart beating against hers were the most romantic things she'd ever experienced. With love filling her heart to bursting, she wrapped her legs around him and brought her mouth to his.

She wasn't sure when the kiss ended. Somewhere in the far reaches of her mind, she heard Kane's raggedly drawn breath, the clink of his belt buckle, the catch in her own breathing. Her eyes closed dreamily, only to open as he made them one. For one brief moment, she thought he was too much man for her, but then he moved, and her body gave and shifted, sounds she didn't recognize as her own forming in the back of her throat. There was no music, and yet she was sure she could hear a throbbing rhythm, a crooning melody. Little by little, a smile of wonder found its way to her mouth.

"Oh, Kane." His features were always striking. In passion, they were even more rugged and sharply honed. His lips were set, his teeth clenched, his eyes partly closed. She wanted to tell him to be careful of his shoulder, but he started to move, and she moaned, instead.

She'd grown accustomed to the butterfly wings that had taken to fluttering low in her belly, but when they brushed her breasts and tingled at every pulse point, she gave up all conscious thought and cried out her response. His release followed hers, his movements slowing and finally stilling completely. He took a shuddering breath, his eyes opening, the expression in their depths hazy and intimate and sensual.

Josie didn't think she would ever tire of looking at his face. Emotions quaked in her chest, her eyes brimming with tears. "If this is how it's always going to be when you come home," she whispered, her face level with his, "I'm not going to mind you leaving quite so much."

Kane's heart was beating fast, his breathing was still ragged, his mind still fuzzy. When his eyes focused, he found himself staring at the curl of Josie's eyelashes, the curve of her smile. Her lips were kiss-swollen, her gray eyes brimming with serenity and intelligence. Wiggling slightly, she wrapped her arms around his neck and hugged him, her breasts taut against his chest. Normally it took a little time for a man's body to rejuvenate. Yet he felt himself responding all over again.

"Am I getting heavy?" she whispered.

"You're a featherweight."

She tipped her head at an irreverent angle and said, "I think you like me this way. And one of these days you're going to admit that you're glad Daddy and the boys forced you to marry me.''

Kane lowered her feet to the floor very, very slowly. As if oblivious to the sudden change in him, she stepped out of his arms and deftly snatched her shirt from the nail that had snagged it earlier. The burning in his lungs reminded him to breathe, and brought him to his senses. He righted his own clothing by rote, his thoughts chugging in perfect time to his heart. He remembered walking through the door and finding Josie bent over her birdhouses, but he couldn't quite remember how he'd gone from watching her to making love to her. Damn. That shouldn't have happened, but no matter what she said, he wasn't happy about the fact that he'd been forced to marry her.

The sex was good. Sex always was. Kane knew better than to get used to the good things in life. And he would never become too attached.

''Something tells me you and I are going to be doing a lot of fighting in the years to come,'' Josie was saying. ''I talked to Daddy today, and he said as long as we always kiss and make up, that isn't a bad thing. Back on the mountain, Edwina Gilson has been throwing things at her husband, Raymond, for years. She hit him with a vase one time. It took five stitches to put his forehead back together. He hasn't lost his whole paycheck in a poker game since then, and she's learned to aim a little to the right of her target. It's worked out pretty well, all in all. Why, they'll be celebrating their thirty-seventh wedding anniversary this fall. What do you think we'll look like when we've been married that long?''

''Josie.''

There was something in the tone of Kane's voice that made Josie glance up at him. His eyes were sharp and assessing, and bore into her. She searched for a plausible explanation for the sudden severity in his expression. Swallowing with difficulty, she found her voice. "You're not going to head out on another bounty hunt, are you?"

The shake of his head only made her more uneasy.

"I don't want you to get the wrong idea about what just happened."

Unable to keep the quaver out of her voice, she asked, "What would you say is the right idea?"

He raked his fingers through his hair, and suddenly, she thought he looked tired. "This was nice, but I think you should know—"

"Nice?"

"You know what I—"

"*Nice!*" she repeated, her voice rising. "I'll have you know it was a lot better than *nice.*"

"All right," he said tentatively, as if testing the idea. "It was better than nice. But it doesn't change the fact that I went to see that attorney in Butte again earlier today. Everything is in order. Divorce papers will be arriving soon."

"But there's no need to get a divorce, Kane. Don't you see? What just happened between us proves that we can work this out."

"What just happened proves that we're human. But there's nothing to work out." He started toward the door.

"That's it?" she asked, hating the pattern she saw forming. "That's all you have to say?"

He turned slowly, and heaved a huge sigh. "Don't expect more from me than I can give."

His words held warning. Before she could ask him what he was warning her against, he strode out the door. She heard the Jeep sputter to life. Holding her shirt closed with one hand, she followed him outside. She wanted to tell him to get his butt back here, but some advice Gwen had given her days ago kept her still. Keep him off balance. Do the last thing he would expect.

"Kane?" she called.

He glanced at her, his eyes narrowing.

"What time will you be home for supper?"

His surprise was evident in the arch of his eyebrows and the way he held his mouth. Josie held perfectly still, doing everything in her power to keep her nerves from showing. He reached for his cowboy hat lying on the seat next to him then peered out over the horizon. Cramming his hat on his head, he said, "I don't know what you're up to, but—"

"You know what your problem is?" she called. "You're too suspicious. Supper will be ready at six-thirty."

Turning on her heel, she strode back into the tack room and started her saw. The next time she looked, the Jeep was a speck on the horizon.

"I had a long talk with Gwen this afternoon—let's see, what else do we need? A spoon for the brussels sprouts and the bottle of low-fat dressing. No, no, you must be tired after chasing all those nasty bail hoppers and then working on the ranch this afternoon. You stay right where you are. I'll get them."

While Josie spun away as if she were a cyclone, Kane sank onto his chair. She was back seconds later, a spoon in one hand, a bottle in the other, picking up her one-sided conversation without missing a beat.

"Honestly, I don't know how she does it."

For a second Kane thought, Who? But then he remembered Josie was talking about Gwen.

"She says she goes days on end without talking to another living soul other than Melissa, Mallory and Spence. She even went so far as to say she *likes* the quiet and solitude out here. She claims there's an energy, like a pulse, that rolls out of the mountains and trembles over the plains. She says that once it takes hold of you, it never lets go. Do you think that's true?''

Running a hand over the whisker stubble on his chin, Kane could only shrug. Josie dished a spoonful of something green and smelly onto his plate and said, ''If there really is a pulse, it hasn't gotten ahold of you, because you leave all the time. What's the matter? Don't you like brussels sprouts?''

Kane nudged one of them with his fork and almost shuddered.

''Why aren't you eating your supper?''

Is that what she called this? Supper? Along with the *brussels sprouts,* she'd prepared a salad topped with cheese that had a funny aftertaste and salad dressing that had a funny texture. A bed of rice covered with something low in fat, low in sodium and low in flavor made up the main course.

Pushing his plate away, he said, ''If this is your way of getting even, it's working.''

Josie sat back. Staring at Kane, she pushed her own plate away from her. He'd shown up for supper, washed his hands and otherwise skirted her as if he were a cat who'd found its way into a dog kennel. At five feet two, a hundred and five pounds, she wasn't what she would call intimidating. So it wasn't *her* he was afraid of. What was it? Love? Happiness? Good health?

It made her all the more certain he needed her, and all the more dedicated to finding a way to his heart. She knew he had a heart. It was evident in the way he'd hunkered down to look at the new kittens Mallory and Melissa had shown him when he'd first pulled into the driveway at a few minutes past six-thirty. It was in his voice whenever he talked to Spence, and in his eyes when he listened to Gwen. Yes, he definitely had a heart. He just didn't want anyone to know it.

Chest brimming with emotion, she said, "No matter what you think, I'm not trying to get even with you for anything. I got this recipe from a television show. Your cholesterol level must be through the roof, but if you don't like green vegetables and steamed chicken, what do you want to eat?"

He jumped to his feet and paced to the sink. "What are you doing, Josie?"

"I'm making small talk."

"Why?"

"It's what people do. What's the matter? Don't you like me to talk to you, either?"

Kane covered his eyes with his hand and slowly shook his head. "I don't want to hurt you, and that's what's going to happen if you stay here. You'll convince yourself that you really do love me, and that you're attached to me. And that's going to make it harder on you when the divorce papers arrive."

That was her Kane, always thinking of others. She sashayed closer, her heart beating a steady rhythm, his eyes narrowing with every step she took. She reached up on tiptoe and laid a hand to his cheek. "You seem to have a definite problem with commitment. Believe me, you've done everything a man can do to warn a woman. If I get hurt, I'll handle it. And if you insist upon going through with the divorce, I'll have no choice but to handle that, as well. But until then, this is where I want to be. I know you aren't much for creature comforts, but can't you simply allow yourself to enjoy this for however long it lasts?"

Kane stared at her, dumbfounded. He knew what was best. She wouldn't listen. To enjoy this for however long it lasted was the equivalent of playing Russian roulette. It was emotional suicide.

"You aren't going to leave of your own free will, are you?"

She shook her head ever so slowly.

Kane gritted his teeth. On a bounty hunt, he knew when to step out of the shadows, and when to turn tail and run. Applying the same tactics to his personal life, he reached for his hat and headed for the door. Out in the barn, he saddled up his favorite horse, swung into the saddle and rode away to check on some fences that needed mending. Somewhere. Galloping over Slater land, he vowed to find a way to convince Josie that leaving was for her own good.

Except for the light Josie had left on for him in the kitchen, the bunkhouse was dark and quiet when Kane went back inside shortly after midnight. Until a few weeks ago it had smelled dank and musty whenever he returned. Now, he smelled something different every time he walked through the door. Supper lingered in the air tonight, reminding him he hadn't eaten. There were peaches in a bowl on the table, and wildflowers in a jelly jar near the sink. Little by little Josie was turning his bunkhouse into a home. The thought made his stomach knot and burn.

He fixed himself a cold chicken sandwich, and ate it standing up. Next, he stood beneath the shower for a long time, letting the hot water pummel his shoulders, steam curling all around him. He'd done a lot of thinking while he'd ridden the fences. He'd discovered two places that needed mending, and he'd faced the fact that Josie wasn't going to leave without a very good reason. He was going to have to explain to her why he wasn't husband material, and why he couldn't change. It was going to involve dredging up the past, something he enjoyed as much as a bullet ripping through his shoulder. But it had to be done. The sooner the better.

He turned off the shower, dried with a towel he didn't recognize and strode into his bedroom, fully prepared to confront Josie. His steps slowed the instant he saw her slight form underneath the covers. Stopping at the foot of the bed, he called her name.

She made a humming sound, but she didn't awaken. He stood watching her for a long time, thinking she even sings in her sleep. Her face looked pale in the moonlight, her hair spread over her pillow. He'd never known anyone who slept as soundly as her. Deciding their confrontation would have to wait, he crawled beneath the sheets. After a long time, he closed his eyes.

Kane breathed deeply and moaned softly. He was either dreaming, or he was being nudged awake by soft kisses and warm, smooth hands that made his skin prickle and desire uncurl a little more with every touch. Rolling to his back, he opened his eyes, sucking in a ragged breath as Josie's hand encircled him.

Josie.

The sky outside the window was the hazy gray of pre-dawn, Josie's eyes a deeper, darker shade. "Good morning," she whispered, stretching provocatively on top of him.

He'd come to several conclusions out on the range last night. *She moved, straddling him.* Moaning, he tried to pick up his train of thought. He had to talk to her. He had to tell her—

His heart skipped a beat at the feel of her breasts skimming his chest, and he couldn't seem to remember what he'd wanted to say. "Josie, there's something we have to talk about—"

"Shh," she said against his lips. "You told me I talk too much. Remember up in the mountain cabin, when you said you wanted to repay me for saving your life? This is how you can repay me, Kane. By enjoying the time we spend together. I'm a big girl, and I know what I want."

To prove her point, she reached between their bodies. "I saved your life. All I'm asking for in return is a few weeks of your time. Would you give me what I want, Kane?"

There were several things in the world a man could change. It seemed Josie's mind wasn't one of them. But she was right. She was a big girl, a grown woman, with a grown woman's needs. He was only a man. How could he refuse?

He rolled her over so quickly she gasped. Bedsprings creaked, covers rustled. Within moments she was smiling.

Josie wanted to tell him how happy she was. She wanted him to know it went beyond happiness. She was relieved and tickled pink, but his mouth covered hers, and the time for talking came to an end.

Chapter Nine

"Honestly, Kane," Josie declared, putting the sour cream, Colby cheese and bacon into the refrigerator and the ice cream and pork chops into the freezer. "I don't know what will get you first, one of your bail hoppers, or your arteries."

Leaning against the counter in a spot out of her way, Kane crossed his ankles and took another sip of his coffee. It had been three weeks since Josie had insisted she could handle living one day at a time—three of the most pleasure-filled weeks of his life. The woman was every man's fantasy in bed, and a spitfire everywhere else.

They'd just come from the grocery store in Butternut. Josie was putting everything away, talking as usual. He'd tried to help, but had ended up getting in the way. He caught a whiff of her shampoo on one of her treks past him, and a glimpse of her legs through the airy fabric of her skirt. His body perked up despite the fact that it had only been six hours since he'd joined her in the shower.

He wasn't surprised by the fact that he liked having her

in his bed, and he was beginning to get used to her constant chatter and singing. But he was amazed at how much he enjoyed watching her build her birdhouses. The tack room was filled with them—forty-three at last count. She was a genius with a piece of old barn wood and a circular saw. And for someone who didn't finish high school, she had an insuppressible thirst for knowledge. She read anything and everything, from magazines about movie stars, to books, to cereal boxes, to the list of ingredients on the backs of cans. Grocery shopping with her had taken forever.

Their days had settled into a routine of sorts. Josie cooked and chattered and built her birdhouses, and Kane helped Spence on the ranch, exercised his right arm and waited for his next bounty hunt. His last job had only taken two days. When he'd arrived home, he'd discovered divorce papers lying in the middle of the kitchen table. Neither of them had mentioned the packet. When he'd come in for supper tonight, he'd noticed she'd placed them on top of the refrigerator, in plain view, but out of their way. Kane supposed he should broach the subject, but as far as he was concerned, as long as she didn't expect too much out of this relationship, or try to get too close, those papers could stay there indefinitely.

"...Daddy says Tyler is finally potty trained. Now if only he could make that much progress with Roy and J.D. They send their regards, by the way."

He finished the rest of his coffee, rinsed the mug out in the sink and waited for her to take a breath. She must have felt his eyes on her, because she paused, a bag of apples in one hand, a tomato in the other. "What?" she asked.

His reaction was swift and instinctive. He'd thought she was plain the first time he saw her. It must have had something to do with the fact that he'd been delirious and half-dead at the time, because there was nothing plain about the color of her hair, her full lips and pert nose, her soft skin and round, gray eyes. In fact, if a man wasn't careful, he could get lost in the expression in those gray eyes.

Kane was very, very careful.

He squared his shoulders and kept his gaze direct. "I talked to Karl Kennedy, the head of the Bail Enforcement Agency in Butte, this afternoon. He has another case for me."

"When?"

"As soon as I can get there." He watched her expression for a telltale glint of hurt or disappointment. Her eyes widened in surprise, but she didn't appear to be resentful or annoyed. She certainly didn't look hurt.

Turning away from him, she opened the refrigerator door and said, "Then I guess I'd better put all the meat in the freezer."

Kane didn't try to deny the pulsing knot that had formed in the very center of him. He could hear Josie crinkling grocery sacks as he strode into the bedroom and tossed a change of clothes into his bag. See? he said to himself. Josie's not the clingy type. She didn't mind being left alone for days on end while he chased criminals. She certainly didn't want more from him than he could give. Reaching for his holster, he glanced at the double bed. Which wasn't a lot. He wished he didn't feel so guilty about that.

All in all, he had it pretty good. He had his brothers and Gwen and the girls, a wife who wasn't afraid to stand up to him, a view of the mountains and another bounty hunt, this one high profile and high risk, waiting for him right now. His life wasn't perfect, but it wasn't half-bad. Glancing at the curtains at the window and the pomander hanging on the peg where his holster had been, he almost smiled. He was probably the only bounty hunter whose gun smelled like lilacs. Tucking the duffel bag under one arm and the holster under the other, he left the room.

Josie heard footsteps behind her, and forbade herself to tremble. She wanted to cry, but she wouldn't. Kane was leaving again. It wasn't the end of the world.

"Well," he said, "I guess I'll see you later."

She wished he would kiss her goodbye, but he never did. Waiting until he reached the door, she said, "Watch your back, Slater. That's bounty hunting talk for *break a leg*."

He looked over his shoulder at her, his face made up of strong lines, his skin stretched taut over high cheekbones and an angular chin. His shoulder was almost completely healed, his skin tanned from the hours he spent out on the range. His eyes were his one feature that could soften his entire appearance. Right now, they were narrowed on her as if he liked what he saw.

Sometimes, when he looked at her this way, his gaze steady, his expression thoughtful, Josie could almost believe he loved her. But then his eyes would take on a deeper glow. Sometimes, he reached for her. Other times he picked a fight. Either way, they ended up in bed, eventually. He handled intimacy very well, doling out pleasure as if he couldn't give her enough. Once, she'd made the mistake of whispering her love for him. He'd waited until he thought she was asleep, then had ridden off on his horse through a rainy mist. In the morning, she'd found a note: "Gone bounty hunting. I don't know when I'll be back."

Josie worried. She ranted. She was terrified for his life. What if he didn't make it back? What if he was injured, bleeding, hurting? He invariably returned, aloof and alone. And they started at square one all over again.

Kane nodded once. Holding his hat between his thumb

and middle finger, he placed it on his head and walked out the door.

Yes, he thought, tossing his duffel bag on the passenger seat. This arrangement could go on indefinitely. Not forever, because nothing lasts forever. But for a while.

In the kitchen, Josie grasped the back of a kitchen chair, listening for Kane's truck to chug to life. I don't know how much longer I can do this, she thought. How long can I tell my heart to be satisfied with a one-sided love affair? How long can I go on talking to myself and deluding myself?

Taking a shuddering breath, she stared out the window at Kane's mountains. They appeared purple, the color of majesty. They made her long for her friendly, green mountains back home. Placing a hand over her heart, she picked up the phone.

Kane made it as far as the end of the driveway when he thought of Gwen and the baby that was due any day. Deciding it might be best to leave Josie a number where he could be reached, he left the truck idling and slipped inside the bunkhouse door.

At first he thought Josie was talking to herself. Before an uncharacteristic smile found its way to his mouth, he realized she was on the phone. Something about the huskiness in her voice held him perfectly still.

"Hi, James... I know I just talked to Daddy this afternoon... No. Nothing's wrong. I just wanted to hear your voice... What? Oh, Kane's fine. He's wonderful... Yes, he just left for another bounty hunt... No, I'm fine, really. It must be the connection... So tell me what's happening on the mountain..."

Kane listened intently. Was it just him, or did her voice sound hollow?

"...Obadiah got a flipper tooth? Really? Why, he's just

like those hockey players we see on TV. James... No... James, for crying out loud, would you listen for half a second... Honestly you're a stubborn one... Yes, I know it takes one to know one..."

No, Kane thought to himself, her voice didn't sound hollow. She was arguing with her brother just as she always did. Everything was okay. For now. Jotting down the phone number for the Bail Enforcement Agency, he glanced at the packet on top of the refrigerator, and slowly backed out of the room.

"Do you want to talk about it?"

Josie turned from the framed photographs she was studying on the mantel and studied Gwen, instead. Her very pregnant, and very *energetic* sister-in-law was on her hands and knees, half in, half out of a narrow closet—the one and only closet on the entire first floor of the old farmhouse.

"Do I want to talk about what?" Josie said to Gwen's backside.

Gwen backed out of the closet, went up on her knees and rolled her eyes in a manner that spoke volumes.

"It's that obvious?" Josie asked.

"That you're worried and lonely?" Gwen shrugged. "It's obvious to me."

Going back to the photographs, Josie said, "I don't want to complain. In many ways, Kane has been wonderful. He's very ardent, very passionate."

"But—"

"But," Josie said, her eyes on an old photo of a much younger Gwen and a woman who looked a lot like her. "I yearn for more of a connection. Not just a sexual connection, but a joining of hearts and hands and souls."

"It took years for Spence and I to form that kind of connection. Are you willing to wait years, Josie?"

Josie didn't see what choice she had. Peering at the smiles on the faces of the two dark-haired women in the photo, she said, "I want to see Kane smile, Gwen."

With an *oomph*, Gwen rose to her feet. "Kane smiles."

Josie made a sound of her own deep in her throat. "I want to see him smile and mean it. And I'd like to understand him."

Eyeing the photograph in Josie's hand, Gwen said, "Has Kane ever mentioned Maggie?"

Hoofbeats sounded in the background, drawing both women to the screen door. Spence and Kane were approaching at a gallop, looking as rugged and wild as cowboys of old. Gray clouds swirled on the horizon behind them, the wind plastering their shirts against their chests.

"Did Kane love this Maggie?" Josie asked.

"Mmm-hmm. You were looking at her picture a few minutes ago. Kane should be the one to tell you about her. If you want to understand him, that might be the place to start."

They walked out onto the porch where Mallory and Melissa were playing with the new kittens. Trepidation skittered up and down Josie's spine. Whatever part this *Maggie* had played in Kane's past, intuition told her she wasn't going to like it.

"Come," Gwen said, sliding a hand around Josie's waist. "Let's take a little walk out to the barn." Turning to her daughters, she said, "Girls, it's time to take the kittens back to their mama. We'll give Rambler and Stalker a drink, and your daddy a kiss."

"Is Aunt Josie going to give Uncle Kane a kiss, too?" Mallory asked.

"I think," Gwen said under her breath, "Aunt Josie was probably thinking more along the lines of leading him into the house by the ear."

* * *

Kane's boots thudded on the ground when he slid from the saddle, his gaze trailing to the gaggle of Slater women who were slowly making their way across the driveway. They made quite a picture: Josie, slight and fair in her oldest pair of jeans and a tank top, Gwen's hair dark, her face rosy, her belly round, Mallory and Melissa trailing behind wearing denim jumpers, a calico kitten tucked underneath each pudgy arm. Maybe it was Josie's laughter that drew his gaze, or maybe it was Josie, herself. The wind blew her hair away from her face, twirling the pale gold strands behind her. She chose that moment to turn her head, her eyes meeting his from the other side of the fence. Her laughter faded, but her smile lingered. He felt a fast little jolt, followed by a rousing dose of pure male attraction.

He'd gotten back from his last bounty hunt a few days ago. He'd watched her intently ever since. She laughed, and talked, and sang, just as she always had. Any strains of sadness must have been in his imagination. The desire pulling at him, however, was very, very real.

He was all set to suggest that the two of them take a leisurely stroll into the bunkhouse when a canary yellow Corvette pulled into the driveway. While Mallory and Melissa skittered into the barn to tuck the kittens into the mother's hiding place behind the feed bin, a tall, exotic-looking woman opened her door and climbed out.

"Excuse me," she called, "but I seem to be lost."

Josie was the first to speak. "My daddy always says as long as you know where you're going, you ain't—aren't—really lost."

"Your daddy sounds like a wise man."

Josie tried not to stare, but it wasn't easy. Somewhere in her thirties, the woman's bright red lips and inch-long auburn hair lit up the plain landscape. She was wearing an orange pantsuit and orange-and-green platform shoes that put her gaze level with Spence's and Kane's.

"I was on my way to Helena to pick up some artwork," she said, "but I must have taken a wrong turn somewhere."

"You're an artist?" Josie asked.

"Helena?" Spence said at the same time.

The woman shook her head at one and nodded at the other. "I'm an art collector, and occasionally an art buyer." She extended her hand to Josie. "My name is—"

"No wait!" Josie exclaimed. "I'd like to guess. Elise."

"No."

"Mercedes."

"Uh-uh."

"Eden."

"Are you kidding?"

"Sasha."

The woman laughed. "You'll never guess in a million years."

"Chantell."

"Josie," Kane grumbled, "let her tell us her name."

"Deidre? Cassandra?"

"It's Sylvia. Sylvia Callahan."

"I would have gotten it," Josie declared, "but it would have taken me a while."

Sylvia Callahan raised two perfectly arched eyebrows and laughed out loud. "You're an artist, aren't you?" Before Josie could argue, Sylvia said, "There's no sense denying it. I can see your aura."

"You can?"

"Josie," Gwen said, nudging her toward the tack room. "Why don't you show Sylvia here your birdhouses?"

Sylvia glanced from Gwen to Josie to the clouds swirling between here and the mountains in the distance. "All right," she said. "I'd love to see your birdhouses. And then, since I would really rather not get stuck on a bridge about to be washed away in that approaching storm, I'd appreciate directions to the nearest high ground.''

Josie's smile was bright. Hell, it was radiant, her eyes sparkling as she looped her arm through the other woman's. A cold knot formed in Kane's stomach. Apprehension gnawed at him. Blaming it on the approaching storm, he excused himself with a nod and a tug at the brim of his hat then led Stalker into the barn. If he would have looked back, he would have known that Josie's eyes were on him until he disappeared from her view.

Josie couldn't sit still.

Sylvia had driven off two hours ago, beating the storm by forty-five minutes. Without her, the ranch seemed even quieter than usual. Josie had been thrilled to pieces when Sylvia had proclaimed that her birdhouses could fetch a hundred dollars or more apiece from folks in the city. But Josie was worried, too. The storm had passed, but another was brewing far back in Kane's eyes.

Don't think about Kane, she told herself. It'll only give you a headache, or a heartache, or both.

Reaching for the lantern, she strode into the hall, and decided to try to think about Sylvia, instead. The woman was amazing. Not only could she see auras, but she'd predicted the severity of the storm right down to the marble-size hail and the driving rain. For all her intuition and insight, she'd been surprised to learn that Kane was a married man.

''That brooding cowboy went to the altar of his own free will?'' she'd asked, tapping one orange-and-green platform shoe.

Josie had shrugged and told her it was a long story.

Sylvia had nodded shrewdly. She was very eccentric. And very perceptive.

Holding the lantern out in front of her, Josie peered into the room she shared with Kane. He'd been quiet and agitated when she'd first come inside. Josie would have liked to attribute it to the change in atmospheric pressure, but she recognized the symptoms of a man gearing up to hightail it out of here. Before he left this time, she intended to ask him one very important question.

She'd jumped at the first crack of thunder, and covered her ears when the hail pummeled the roof as if it were gunfire. Kane had watched the storm from the window, a lethal calmness in his eyes. She'd tried keeping up a one-sided conversation, talking about Sylvia and Gwen and anything else she could think of. Her own unease made the conversation seem stilted. She had to ask about Maggie. But how?

Spence had shown up at the door before Josie had come close to broaching the subject, and the Slater brothers had ridden off to check on the herd and the damage left by the storm. Josie planned to be ready for Kane when he returned. She would hog-tie him if she had to, but she was going to get to the bottom of the truth if she had to wait all night.

Josie didn't have to wait nearly that long for Kane to return. She heard him ride in shortly after nine. He must have unsaddled Stalker in record time, because Kane was inside the bunkhouse within minutes, his boots soggy, his hat dripping, his eyes distant.

She was all set to blurt out her first question, but her gaze followed him as he stalked to the refrigerator and reached for the packet lying on top.

"What are you doing?" she asked.

He removed his hat and slowly pushed the divorce papers toward Josie. "It's for your own good. You're unhappy here. You're lonely. Admit it."

Josie didn't know whether to cry or slug him. She twirled around, pacing to the counter, to the edge of the table, to the doorway leading down the narrow hall. Turning, she fixed him with a wide-eyed stare. "That's your answer to our problem? Just sign on the dotted line?"

Across the room, Kane watched Josie with a practiced, leery eye. Her voice had been deep and edged in control. It reminded him of the Chinook winds that blew down from the eastern slopes in winter. The warm, dry air melted the snow, luring everyone outside with the promise of spring. A raging blizzard invariably followed.

Eyes trained on Josie, who was slowly striding closer, Kane braced himself for the cold.

There was nothing cold about the brush of her lips on his, the flick of her tongue, or the way she murmured his name. He never saw the kiss coming. One second her eyes had been on his. The next thing he knew she swooped up on tiptoe and stole his breath away. His heart chugged, his arms going around her, pulling her hard against him, his body reacting, his mind reeling, something in his hand fluttering to the floor.

"Why did you do that?" he rasped.

"Because," she whispered, her fingers already on the last button on his shirt. "This is the only way we seem to be able to connect, and I think we both need a connection right now, don't you?"

He pulled her shirt from the waistband of her jeans, and molded her more firmly to the contours of his body. Rain pattered the roof, and somewhere far, far away, someone called his name.

It was Josie who ended the kiss, Josie who was the first

to come to her senses. "That's Spence's voice," she whispered.

"Kane, Josie!" Spence burst through the screen door, his hair and shirt wet from the rain.

"Spence, what's wrong?" Kane and Josie said at once.

"It's Gwen. The baby's coming. The power's out, and there's no time to make it to town. Come quick. I need your help."

Chapter Ten

Josie grabbed the lantern and hurried out the door, Spence and Kane right behind her. She paid no heed to the water puddles in the driveway, not stopping until she'd set foot inside the big house's front door. Normally bustling with activity and noise and scents, the house was dark and silent and smelled of rain.

"Gwen?" Josie called.

"This way," Spence said, leading them into the main bedroom in the back of the house.

Josie assessed the situation with one sweeping glance. The girls were huddled on the bed next to their mother, crying. Gwen's face looked pale in the flicker of lantern light, and was contorted in pain.

"So you've decided to have the baby at home," Josie said, breezing closer.

The contraction must have eased a little, because Gwen breathed deeply and tried to smile.

"How long has this been going on?" Josie asked.

Spence spoke up behind her. "Her water broke half an

hour ago. It's been nonstop since then. I put a call in to the doctor over the CB, but there's a bridge out over the Whitewater River. There's no telling how long it would take us to drive into Butternut by another route.''

"It doesn't matter," Gwen said, finally speaking. "This baby doesn't want to wait through a car ride to Butternut."

Another contraction came out of the blue. Gwen was right. This baby was going to be born right here, and from the looks of things, soon.

The girls were crying again. Spence didn't look much better. Taking Gwen's hand, Josie said, "Don't worry, honey, Josie's here. Spence, I'm going to need some clean sheets and several towels. Mallory and Melissa, I want you to show Uncle Kane where your mama keeps her candles. When he's finished putting a candle in every room, I want you to help him make sandwiches. He's real, real hungry, so make a bunch."

The girls jumped up and skittered off the bed. "Come on, Uncle Kane," Mallory, the older of the two, said. "Mama keeps a whole box of candles in the kitchen."

Gwen moaned again, stopping Kane's and Spence's footsteps in the doorway. "Do you know how to deliver a baby?" Spence asked.

Josie swallowed the lump in her throat and pasted a smile on her face. "Don't worry. I've seen it on TV a dozen times. Now go on, you two. Hop to it. I need those sheets, and this baby doesn't want to be born in the dark."

Kane and Spence shared a long look. They'd both delivered dozens of colts and calves over the years, but this was different. Gwen seemed more fragile, her pain more real. As if on cue, they turned on their heels and did as Josie instructed.

Half an hour later the entire first floor was glowing beneath the soft light of a dozen candles. Mallory and Melissa had made enough sandwiches to feed an army, and enough mess for a dozen children. Spence was in the bedroom with his wife, and Kane was wandering from room to room, his heart beating, his nerves having a roping contest in his stomach. Every now and then, Gwen cried out. Josie's voice, ever calm and soothing, crooned words of encouragement.

And then, as if someone flipped a switch, everything became utterly silent. Eerily silent. Mallory and Melissa must have noticed, because they melted into Kane's side, tucking a small hand into each of his. Finally, after what seemed like forever, a baby's tiny cry wavered to their ears.

The girls darted down the hall. By the time Kane arrived in the doorway, Josie was handing a red-face baby wrapped up in a checkered kitchen towel into Gwen's outstretched arms.

"It's a girl." There were tears in Josie's voice, and a smile of wonder on her face.

"Spence," Gwen whispered weakly. "I think this one's gonna have your eyes."

The girls, suddenly shy, hung back near the foot of the bed. "Come closer," Spence called, his own voice emotion-filled and husky. "Come meet your baby sister."

Curious and uncertain, they climbed onto the bed for a closer look at the baby.

"Do you mind that it's not a boy?" Gwen asked.

It was Spence who answered. "How could we mind? We have the best family in the world."

Tears ran down Josie's face at the pride and wonder and love in Spence's eyes. "What are you going to name her?" she asked.

Gwen and Spence shared a long look. "We were thinking of naming her Maggie," Gwen said softly.

The room fell silent as all eyes turned to Kane. "How would you feel about that?" Spence asked.

Kane's expression was made up of so many emotions Josie couldn't name them all. He'd backed as far away as he could get without actually leaving the room, his face as pale as it had been the night he'd fallen into her cabin, hurt and bleeding, nearly two months ago. "It's your baby," he said. "Name her whatever you like."

Without another word, he left, a knowing look passing between Spence and Gwen. It seemed Josie was the only one not in on the secret. The baby began to cry, Gwen crooned and Spence and the girls huddled close by. Feeling like an outsider, Josie went out to the kitchen on the pretense of getting the new mother something cool to drink.

She covered the stacks of sandwiches with plastic wrap, tidied up the kitchen, then carried four glasses of juice into the bedroom. She checked on Gwen and the baby two more times. When Doc Jenkins finally arrived, Josie excused herself and went in search of Kane.

She found him in their bedroom, stuffing clothes into his worn duffel bag. Pausing in the doorway, she said, "Going someplace?"

He looked up, the double bed between them, his eyes cool and remote. She strolled into the room, then stood at the foot of the bed, grappling to find the right words. "It's been quite a night."

He zipped the bag with one brisk tug.

"They won't name the baby Maggie if you don't want them to, Kane."

His gaze delved hers for so long she thought he was going to tell her what he was thinking, what he was feeling, what he was afraid of. As if catching himself in the nick of time, he straightened and headed for the door.

"It's been an emotion-filled night," Josie whispered. "You don't have to leave."

He stopped at the door, but he didn't turn around. "Yes, I do."

Fed up with wishing and wanting and trying to understand, she planted her hands on her hips and sputtered, "I could use some answers, and I'd just as soon not wait for you to mosey back home after you've put another big, bad felon behind bars. I know you once loved someone named Maggie. And it's not so unusual for a man who's been single for thirty-four years to have a little trouble adjusting to married life. My daddy was almost that old when he—"

In a voice almost too quiet to hear, he said, "I wasn't single all my thirty-four years, Josie."

The room had grown so quiet Josie wondered if she was the only one who could hear her heart beating. "You were married before?"

He turned slowly, a slight hesitation in his hawklike eyes. A primitive warning sounded in her brain, and suddenly, she didn't think she was up to coping with whatever he was going to say. Grasping the iron bed frame so tight her knuckles turned white, she closed her eyes and waited.

"You're right," Kane said, his voice catching. "Her name was Maggie. We were married for three years."

Three years. A flash of grief ripped through Josie. She'd known she hadn't been Kane's first lover, but she'd thought she was his first wife. Something told her Kane hadn't been dragged, kicking and screaming to the altar the first time. A sob stuck sideways in her throat. Forcing it back down, she said, "Where is Maggie now?"

"She's buried in a little country cemetery next to my mother and my father."

For once in her life, Josie couldn't think of a thing to say. She didn't ask any more questions, or utter any empty words of condolence for the loss of a woman she'd never known, a woman Kane had once loved, and probably loved still. The fact that he had never told her about Maggie made this revelation more poignant, more staggering.

Suddenly Josie understood why he took so many chances with his life. He wasn't simply tempting fate. He was making sure he wouldn't be around the next time somebody he loved died.

He cleared his throat. "I have to go, Josie. I talked to Karl hours ago, before Gwen went into labor. He's expecting me."

She nodded. "If you have to go, you have to go."

"Will you be all right?"

"I'm a big girl. If I could doctor a gunshot wound during a raging blizzard and deliver a baby during a power outage, I think I can take care of myself."

He looked at her one more time. Unable or unwilling—Josie would never know which—to say what was on his mind, he reached for his holster and left.

Her senses were so finely tuned she heard the click of the door as he let himself out. When the sound of Kane's truck had faded in the distance, she released the death grip she had on the iron bed frame and walked from one room to the next. She wasn't certain why she strode outside. Finding herself out by the fence Spence and Kane had mended a few weeks ago, she peered into the distance. The rain had let up, but the moon and stars were still hiding above the clouds. The sun would probably be out tomorrow. Tomorrow, Josie was going to have to decide what to do.

Kane downshifted and slammed on the brakes. His tires slid over loose gravel, coming to a stop inches away from Jud Harlow's small herd of cattle. The Herefords bawled at the interruption as if Kane was the one in the wrong place, not them. He honked his horn, swearing under his breath as they lumbered across the road in their own sweet time. The minute they cleared the other side, he jammed the lever into a higher gear and sped off toward home.

He'd been gone for four days, and he'd been uneasy every minute of it. He'd done a lot of thinking while he'd been waiting for his latest felon to make his move, and a lot of remembering. He'd thought nothing could daunt Josie. Not gunshot wounds, not even delivering babies beneath the flicker of candlelight. Why, then, was he having so much trouble getting the glimmer of tears he'd seen in her eyes out of his mind?

He prodded his truck to go faster, relieved to finally see Slater land. The check in his pocket was large enough to live on for a year or more. He'd been thinking about slowing down a little, maybe taking the rest of the year off. Who knows? Maybe he could be content to work on the ranch and listen to Josie talk.

It was dusk when he pulled up in front of his place. Over in the big house, the new baby was crying at the top of her healthy little lungs. He remembered when Mallory and Melissa had cried like that. He planned to mosey on over there later and hold her and find out what Spence and Gwen had ended up naming her. First, he had to see Josie, to touch her, and take her to bed.

He'd been wrong to leave with everything so unsettled. He would make it up to her. *If she let him.*

Ignoring the apprehension crawling down his spine, he opened the door. The first thing he noticed was the silence. It took him a minute to figure out that the curtains Josie had hung at the windows were missing. With his misgivings increasing by the second, he headed for their bedroom. Everything was as neat as a pin. The bed was made, but the usual jelly jar of flowers was gone. And so were Josie's clothes.

He strode out to the kitchen and opened the refrigerator as if by rote, swallowing at the sight of eggs, cheese, sour cream, a raw, thick T-bone steak, all the foods Josie had claimed would kill him someday. He went out to the tack room next. The sight awaiting him there left him feeling hollow and empty. The birdhouses were gone.

It took a cramp in his right hand and an ache in his jaw to remind him to unclench his teeth and uncurl his fist. A cold shiver worked over him. Other than barn wood stacked neatly along one wall, there was no sign that Josie had ever been there.

He ran a hand over his eyes, down across the whisker stubble on his cheeks and chin. Imposing an iron will upon himself, he left the empty tack room, telling himself Josie's leaving was for the best. He would have his peace and quiet back. And he wouldn't have to worry.

Worry ate at Kane. He was sitting on the fence in the gathering darkness, practicing his lassoing skills, scowling. He'd been back for a week. At first, he'd blamed the knot in his stomach on guilt. By the third day he'd started to wonder if maybe Josie had been right and all the red meat he ate was damaging his heart. He'd told Josie he didn't have a heart. Come to find out, he'd had a heart all along. It had just been numb. It wasn't numb anymore.

He hoped she was all right. How could she be all right? She talked to strangers. She used power tools. She opened her door to men who were bleeding.

Night had fallen by the time he came out of his reverie. It was nearing the middle of May, and although the days were warm, nights were still chilly. His father used to call this good sleeping weather. Kane knew he needed to sleep.

But any decent amount of sleep had been eluding him for the past seven days.

Lights were on in the big house. Kane could imagine Spence and Gwen moving around inside, discussing bottoming out beef prices, sharing a smile as they tucked the girls into bed. Other than asking Kane if he could take over on the ranch for a few days so he could help Gwen with the girls, Spence hadn't said much about Josie's departure. Kane figured there wasn't much to say. She'd given the marriage her best shot. It hadn't worked out, so she'd left. He didn't blame her one bit.

She'd been out to the ranch to visit. Mallory and Melissa had spilled the beans while they'd been playing with the new kittens a few days ago. That meant Josie wasn't hitchhiking back to Tennessee. She was safe, somewhere in the area, which made it pretty hard to go on pretending the knot in his chest was from plain and simple worry.

Taking a cigarette out of its package, Kane thought there had never been anything plain *or* simple about Josie.

Emotions churned inside him, pressing against his chest, pushing at him from every direction. Jumping down from the fence, he grabbed his cowboy hat off his head and ran a hand through his hair. The action did nothing to relieve his pent-up nerves and crippling frustration. Normally he would have been on his way to Butte and another assignment long before it got this bad. His window would have been down, dust curling behind his truck as he sped away.

He'd taken Stalker out for a midnight run a couple of times, trying to outrun the feelings that were closing in on him. Stalker was the best horse Kane had ever had. As if sensing his rider's frustration, the big, black gelding had galloped over the familiar ground at breakneck speed. Kane had given the horse extra oats and water when they'd returned. After all, it wasn't Stalker's fault the midnight rides seemed to increase Kane's frustration rather than relieve it.

He struck a match, staring at the way it lit up the night. Moments before the flame reached his fingertips, he extinguished it, crushing the cigarette in his fist.

It was time to stop tempting fate. It was time to stop running.

Kane opened his eyes slowly. His boots creaked as he lowered them from the railing, the metal chair he'd pulled up squeaking in protest to the sudden movement.

He didn't remember falling asleep, but he must have dozed. A baby's cry wafted to his ears. Bowser, who had taken to sleeping over at Kane's place since the arrival of the new baby, whined before settling his snout on his paws once again. The cries grew louder. A light came on in the big house. If Kane could have, he would have smiled. Little Miranda was training her parents well. Peering at that lit window in the distance, he scratched Bowser's head, and slowly rose to his feet.

His boots crunched over loose stones in the driveway, thudding over old floorboards as he let himself into the big house. He stopped short in the curved archway between the living room and the dining room where Josie had danced with Trace. Gwen looked up from the baby at her breast, shaking her head at the way Kane's attention was suddenly trained on the toe of his boot.

"You always were the gentleman in this family," she said quietly.

Kane glanced up in surprise. Ignoring his discomfiture long enough to appreciate the beauty of a mother nursing her child, he thought his brother was a very lucky man. After a long silence, Kane said, "You could have named her Maggie."

Gwen yawned. "Maybe we'll name the next one Maggie. I've already asked Josie to act as our midwife."

"Does Spence know you're already planning a fourth?"

"Don't worry," she said, smiling. "I'll let him in on the secret when the time is right."

"I miss her, Gwen."

Kane didn't know how Gwen knew he was referring to Josie. "Then go to her," she whispered.

"Where is she?"

Shaking her head, Gwen smiled tiredly and said, "I thought you'd never ask." She named a street and house number. "Kane!" she called to his back before he disappeared from view, "it's 3:00 a.m. Don't you think you should wait until daybreak?"

Kane shook his head. There wasn't much a man could do about missing people who had died, but there was something he could do about missing a woman who was very much alive. He only hoped he hadn't waited too long.

Chapter Eleven

Other than a few streetlights, the village of Butternut was dark. Inching through the downtown area, which was called the Four Corners by the townsfolk, Kane startled a pair of mourning doves who were roosting on the town's only Stop sign. He turned right at the end of the street, stopping at the curb in front of the address Gwen had given him. Heart hammering, he slid from the truck, drawn to the back porch light much the way he'd been drawn to the light in that mountain cabin in Tennessee.

The *swish-swish* of sandpaper covered the crunch of his footsteps. Stepping around a bed of bitterroot and poppies, he moved out of the shadows and into a patch of light. A lump came and went in his throat at the sight of Josie leaning over one of her birdhouses. Keeping his voice soft so as not to scare her, he said, "Hello, Josie."

Josie felt the sandpaper beneath her hand, the floorboards beneath her shoes, the cool May night on her arms, but it seemed she could only move her eyes. She didn't want to react to the low timbre in Kane's voice. She especially didn't want her heart to turn over at the gentle, contemplative gleam in his eyes or the deep crease slashing one lean cheek.

She was thankful when he moved, thereby breaking the spell he'd cast over her and enabling her to go back to her latest creation. She heard his boot on the step, and knew he was studying the new birdhouses she'd built.

"What happened to the others?" he asked, his voice low and husky and as dark as secrets whispered in the night.

Resuming her sanding, Josie finally found her voice. "I sold them. Sylvia was right. People in the city are willing to pay a pretty penny for things I used to make for free. Orders are pouring in faster than I can fill them."

"Is that why you're working at four in the morning?"

She paused for a moment. "I couldn't sleep." When he didn't move or reply, she said, "What are you doing here, Kane?"

He turned, and slowly removed his hat. "I've asked myself that question a million times this past week. What *am* I doing here? On this planet, on the ranch, in this life. You see, until I stumbled into your mountain cabin, I thought I knew. I had friends. One or two. I had my brothers, and Gwen and the girls. I had honorable goals and integrity and a soft bed when I wanted it. I thought those things made life worth living. For a long time, I set out to prove it was so. For a long time, it was. But then I met you."

The huskiness in his voice was as rough around the edges as loss. It sent an ache to her heart and tears to her eyes. "I was wrong to force you to marry me, Kane. I guess doing something for the right reasons doesn't make it right. I'm sorry. I signed those divorce papers before I left."

She felt his eyes on her, but she couldn't look up.

"I didn't come here for an apology, Josie. And I sure as hell didn't come here because I want a divorce. No matter what we both thought at the time, you didn't force me to do anything I didn't want to do back in Hawk Hollow. We both know Saxon would have told your brothers to lower their shotguns if I would have asked him to. Going through with that wedding was the first step I took back into the life of the living. Tonight, I'm taking the second step.''

Despite the chill in the air, something went warm deep inside Josie. She couldn't see the color of Kane's eyes through the blur of her tears, but she knew they were light brown, flecked with disappointments from the past and yearnings for the future.

As if he didn't quite trust himself to touch her, he worried the rim of his hat and quietly said, ''I should have told you about Maggie sooner. I've never been able to figure out what people are supposed to say about someone who has died.''

Looking at Kane, a hundred questions went through Josie's mind. He still had the face of an outlaw, two or three days' worth of whisker stubble, a mouth more prone to scowling than smiling. But he wasn't an outlaw. He was just a man. A man who had loved, and lost. Just like everyone else in the world.

Choosing her words very carefully, Josie said, ''She was Gwen's sister, wasn't she?''

Kane nodded, and Josie thought how difficult it must have been for him to lose his wife, when his brother was married to his wife's sister. How tragic for them all. After another long stretch of silence, she said, ''What was she like?''

A muscle worked in his jaw; his throat convulsed on a swallow, but he answered, eventually. ''She was young and pretty and sweet. She never yelled at me, and not once in the three years we were married did I ever hear her sing. She died in a car accident. She wasn't quite twenty-three.''

Josie's vision cleared, along with her heart and throat and mind. She'd learned from experience that there was as much in what Kane didn't say as in what he did say. He didn't mention loving his first wife, but Josie knew he had. He didn't say he loved her—Josie—now, but as he took the few remaining steps separating them, she knew it was true. He stood before her, his heart laying wide-open. And smack-dab in the middle of it, she saw a love as big as his mountains for a woman who liked to laugh and argue and sing.

She smiled. After a time, he did, too.

"Are you going on any more bounty hunts?" she whispered.

He shook his head, a smile creasing one cheek. "I think it's about time I settled down, don't you? And you have to stop buying all those fatty foods. I'm going to need a strong heart if I'm ever going to keep up with you. You're a lot younger than I am, you know."

Josie was almost certain her heart stretched on tiptoe and fluttered in her throat. Of course, it could have been those butterfly wings that had formed the night she'd met Kane. Suddenly she felt as winsome and lithe and free as those flutters. Folding one arm at her waist, she rested her chin in the opposite hand. In a voice purposefully mysterious, she said, "Wasn't it Picasso who said it takes a long time to be young?"

Her laughter drew him closer like the promise of cool shade on a sweltering day. He didn't think he would ever tire of her laugh, or her little snippets of wisdom. As his gaze got stuck on her mouth, he said, "I'm feeling younger all the time. I want us to build a life together, Josie. We could use the money I just earned from my last—and I mean *last*—bounty hunt to buy a different house, maybe one closer to town and people to talk to."

A smile of wonder spread across her face, and she laughed all over again. "We'd better make it a big house because our boys are going to need a lot of room to run."

Kane did a double take. "Our boys?"

She reached for his hand, placing his palm low on her stomach. "The first one is already on his way. I think it's my destiny to be surrounded by wonderful, stubborn men."

Kane felt his eyes widen and his jaw go slack. "You mean?"

Hell, there was only one thing she *could* mean.

"It's why I didn't move back to Hawk Hollow," she whispered. "I decided if I was going to be pining after you for the rest of my life, I might as well do it from here."

Letting out a whoop loud enough to wake the neighbors, Kane swung her off her feet. He didn't know if a woman could tell what sex her unborn child would be, let alone the sex of children not yet conceived, but he knew one thing: He intended to surround her with love for the rest of his life.

Setting her back on her feet, he said, "It looks as if old age is going to run in the family from now on."

"I'm sure our children, not to mention our grandchildren, will be glad to hear that."

"How many children do you see in our future, anyway?"

She tilted her head one way and then the other, as if trying to decide if she dared tell him. With love shining in her eyes and a smile of wonder on her lips, she said, "I thought four, but Sylvia said she saw at least five."

"Five?"

Josie reached for his hand, drawing him inside. "My mama always said it's better to aim for the sky and hit the steeple than to aim for the steeple and hit the mud."

"Ah, Josie?" he whispered after the screen door banged shut behind him. "What are you doing?"

Deftly unfastening the buttons on his shirt, she said, "I'm aiming for the sky, Kane, and I'm shooting for the stars."

Kane closed his eyes against the onslaught of emotions converging in the very center of him. He forced his eyes open again, and there was Josie, looking up at him, waiting. "Which way to the bedroom?" he whispered.

"I thought you said we didn't need a bed."

He moved her hair away from her ear and kissed the soft skin beneath it. "Yes," he whispered huskily, "but you're going to have a baby. Besides, we need a bed for what I have in mind. Did I mention that I love you?"

Tipping her head back, she said, "Oh, Kane. I love you, too. What do you have in mind?"

He whispered his answer into her ear. Her eyebrows rose, a smile spreading across her face. Josie didn't say any more. She simply pointed to the bedroom.

Shoes came off in a tumble, belts and jeans and shirts following close behind. Just as the sky was turning the darkest before dawn, Kane and Josie aimed for the steeple, and reached the stars. Together.

*   *   *   *   *

Sandra Steffen is going back to
BACHELOR GULCH *with her next book. Don't
miss another story in her beloved miniseries,
available in December from Silhouette Romance.
This time, Louetta does get her man!*

HE CAN CHANGE A DIAPER IN THREE SECONDS FLAT BUT CHANGING HIS MIND ABOUT MARRIAGE MIGHT TAKE SOME DOING! HE'S ONE OF OUR

July 1998
ONE MAN'S PROMISE by Diana Whitney (SR#1307)
He promised to be the best dad possible for his daughter. Yet when successful architect Richard Matthews meets C. J. Moray, he wants to make another promise—this time to a wife.

September 1998
THE COWBOY, THE BABY AND THE BRIDE-TO-BE
by Cara Colter (SR#1319)
Trouble, thought Turner MacLeod when Shayla Morrison showed up at his ranch with his baby nephew in her arms. Could he take the chance of trusting his heart with this shy beauty?

November 1998
ARE YOU MY DADDY? by Leanna Wilson (SR#1331)
She hated cowboys, but Marty Thomas was willing to do anything to help her son get his memory back—even pretend sexy cowboy Joe Rawlins was his father. Problem was, Joe thought he might like this to be a permanent position.

Available at your favorite retail outlet, only from

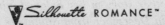

twins
on the doorstep

BY STELLA BAGWELL

The Murdocks are back!
All the adorable children from the delightful
Twins on the Doorstep
miniseries are grown up and
finding loves of their own.

You met Emily in
THE RANCHER'S BLESSED EVENT
(SR #1296, 5/98)
and in August 1998 Charlie is the
lawman about to be lassoed in

THE RANGER AND THE WIDOW WOMAN
(SR#1314)

In the next few months look for Anna's and Adam's
stories—because the twins are also heading for the altar!

Only in

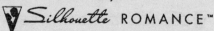 *Silhouette* ROMANCE™

Available at your favorite retail outlet.

HERE COME THE
Virgin Brides!

Celebrate the joys of first love with more unforgettable stories from Romance's brightest stars:

SWEET BRIDE OF REVENGE
by Suzanne Carey—June 1998 (SR #1300)

Reader favorite Suzanne Carey weaves a sensuously powerful tale about a man who forces the daughter of his enemy to be his bride of revenge. But what happens when this hard-hearted husband falls head over heels...for his wife?

THE BOUNTY HUNTER'S BRIDE
by Sandra Steffen—July 1998 (SR #1306)

In this provocative page-turner by beloved author Sandra Steffen, a shotgun wedding is only the beginning when an injured bounty hunter and the sweet seductress who'd nursed him to health are discovered in a remote mountain cabin by her gun-toting dad and *four* brothers!

SUDDENLY...MARRIAGE!
by Marie Ferrarella—August 1998 (SR #1312)

RITA Award-winning author Marie Ferrarella weaves a magical story set in sultry New Orleans about two people determined to remain single who exchange vows in a mock ceremony during Mardi Gras, only to learn their bogus marriage is the real thing....

And look for more VIRGIN BRIDES in future months, only in—

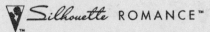 *Silhouette* ROMANCE™

Available at your favorite retail outlet.

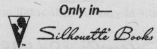

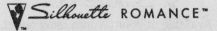

The World's Most Eligible Bachelors are about to be named! And Silhouette Books brings them to you in an all-new, original series....

World's Most Eligible Bachelors

Twelve of the sexiest, most sought-after men share every intimate detail of their lives in twelve never-before-published novels by the genre's top authors.

Don't miss these unforgettable stories by:

Dixie Browning

MARIE FERRARELLA

Jackie Merritt

Tracy Sinclair

BJ James

RACHEL LEE

Suzanne Carey

Gina Wilkins

VICTORIA PADE

MAGGIE SHAYNE

Anne McAllister

Susan Mallery

Look for one new book each month in the **World's Most Eligible Bachelors** series beginning September 1998 from Silhouette Books.

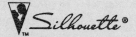

Silhouette®

Available at your favorite retail outlet.